David Marcus was born in Cork and is a graduate of University College, Cork, and King's Inns, Dublin. He practised at the Irish Bar for some years before founding and editing the prestigious *Irish Writing*. After thirteen years in London, he returned to Dublin where he started the weekly *New Irish Writing* page in the Irish Press, which has since become a national institution. Married to the writer Ita Daly, David Marcus retired as Literary Editor of the *Irish Press* in 1986 to devote more time to writing. His first novel *Next Year in Jerusalem* was published in 1954 and since then he has had many stories and poems published in Ireland, Britain and America and has edited numerous anthologies of Irish short stories. *A Land Not Theirs* and *A Land in Flames* were both published by Corgi.

Also by David Marcus

A LAND NOT THEIRS
A LAND IN FLAMES

and published by Corgi Books

Who Ever Heard of an Irish Jew?

David Marcus

CORGI BOOKS

WHO EVER HEARD OF AN IRISH JEW?

A CORGI BOOK 0 552 13625 5

Originally published in Great Britain by Bantam Press,
a division of Transworld Publishers Ltd.

PRINTING HISTORY
Bantam Press edition published 1988
Corgi edition published 1990

'Sonny Boy', De Sylva, Brown, Henderson, Jolson used by kind permission of
Redwood Music Ltd., 14 New Burlington Street, London W1X 2LR.

This book is set in 10/11 pt English Times
by Colset Private Limited, Singapore.

Corgi Books are published by Transworld Publishers Ltd.,
61–63 Uxbridge Road, Ealing, London W5 5SA, in Australia
by Transworld Publishers (Australia) Pty. Ltd., 15–23 Helles
Avenue, Moorebank, NSW 2170, and in New Zealand by
Transworld Publishers (N.Z.) Ltd., Cnr. Moselle and
Waipareira Avenues, Henderson, Auckland.

Made and printed in Great Britain by
Cox & Wyman Ltd., Reading, Berks.

To the memory of my parents

Acknowledgements

Some of these stories, either in their present form or in an earlier version, first appeared in *Winter's Tales from Ireland*, the *Irish Press* 'New Irish Writing', the *Jewish Chronicle*, the *Jewish Quarterly*, and *Cara*.

Contents

Who Ever Heard of an Irish Jew?

I knew the question she was on the point of asking and I guessed from the way she carried her big bust that she wouldn't be worried about offending me. Her busy fingers paused before reluctantly drawing a card from the box on her desk. Then, briskly, in a no-nonsense voice, she accused:

'You're sure you *are* Jewish?'

Momma, would I have borne the name of Cohen for twenty years if I hadn't been a Jew? I wondered how I could prove my authenticity to her – apart from one particular way that would hardly further my cause (though who could tell?).

'I mean,' she grated on, 'we never had an *Irish* Jew before. And you don't *sound* Jewish.' Perhaps I should tell her the joke about the two Chinese Jews. (One Chinese Jew met another Chinese Jew. Dialogue: 'You Jlewish?' 'Yes, I'm Jlewish. And you?' 'Yes, I'm Jlewish too.' 'Funny – you don't look Jlewish.') For God's sake, what would I be doing in the Jewish Sabbath Observance Employment Bureau if I were a *goy*?

But she was as sharp at answering questions – even unspoken ones – as she was at asking them. 'We *do* get a few non-Jews here, you know. It's quite an attraction to them to pretend to be Jewish if it means a job in an Orthodox Jewish business house – no Saturday work, early closing on Fridays in the winter and all Jewish holidays off. As well as the normal national holidays. We *do* have to be careful.'

'Of course,' I said.

When it didn't appear that I was going to come up with

anything more helpful, she suggested, 'Perhaps you have some proof of identification with you?'

My face lit up at the thought. To her I must have seemed even more stupid than I really was, but it was just that the pace of London had thrown me. I had only been a week there – my first time outside Ireland – and I was still catching flies.

'I got this this morning,' I said over-eagerly, drawing my mother's letter from my pocket and pushing it under her nose.

She looked at it impassively but made no effort to take it in her hand.

I felt like telling her that she was welcome to read it too if she still didn't believe I was Jewish. One paragraph would have been enough to convince her (Make sure the sheets aren't damp, eat regular meals, keep away from Soho, and had I made any friends yet? – i.e., met any nice Jewish girls).

'It's from my mother,' I explained encouragingly, eyeing the big bust and thinking she must have *some* maternal instincts I could arouse. But she continued to gaze coolly at the envelope.

'What a curious stamp,' was the only response as she withdrew her face.

'It's Irish,' I said, and immediately blushed at the obviousness of my remark. Then, realizing she might think I was implying that one could not expect an Irish postage stamp to be anything but artistically inadequate, I blushed again.

She allowed herself a wintry smile which she tried to hide by examining a non-existent speck of dust on her bosom. Then it was back to business.

'How is your maths?' Tonelessly, her eyes riveted on the filing card in her hand.

'Oh, very good,' I assured her. 'I kept all the books in my father's business. And I got a hundred and five per cent in the Intermediate Examination for maths.'

She raised a slow stare and I knew I had said something wrong again.

'Sorry. I should have explained,' I quickly added. 'The Inter is a big national exam. All the Irish schools do it.'

There was a solid pause. What now?

'One hundred and *five* per cent? In maths?'

She seemed shaken. Obviously *all* my credentials were suspect. I was about to tell her that the extra 5 per cent was for answering the paper in Irish but she waved me aside.

'Go to these people,' she said, writing out an address for me. 'They're looking for an accounts clerk.' I thanked her. 'You may just suit them,' she added. There was no hint of sarcasm in her voice but that expressive bosom jerked up like two massive eyebrows raised in doubt. Small wonder – as I left her office I suddenly realized that I wasn't wearing a hat. Imagine! An Orthodox Jew with his head uncovered! I could guess what she was thinking: what can you expect from the Irish?

Levin Brothers Limited was a six-storey warehouse in the heart of London. Heart! More like guts. It employed over 200 people – all Jews except for the packers and porters – and that was more Jews under one roof than the whole community I had lived in all my life. There I met – and was prissily ignored by – Jewish girls with names like Sonia and Clarice and Petula, and the men were Rodney or Cyril or Dale. I was the only Joe, but not at first. At first I was nothing, then after a few weeks I was, stiffly, Mr Cohen, and later still someone started to call me Joe. But by then I had already explored the lower orders down as far as the packing department in the basement and was relieved to meet throughout my descent with acceptance – of a sort. I was immediately nicknamed 'Shamus', asked if the Irish Jews went to *shul* on St Patrick's Day and spoken to in Yiddish so that my Yiddish-with-a-brogue replies could be savoured. But at least that was more to my liking than the toffee-nosed primness of the sixth floor. Most congenial of all was the basement, and there I took to spending my lunch breaks, where those who didn't eat out brought their parcels of sandwiches and brewed tea. Among the gossip and card-playing I could at least discuss home (i.e., Irish) affairs with the many expatriate packers. And there too I was able to talk with Gary.

I met Gary the first day he started at Levin's. I was in the third-floor stockroom, checking an invoice with Issy Kernick, when the service lift came up from the basement and eased to a stop. The truck on it was loaded with refrigerators and the lift had halted at least two inches below the stockroom floor. Any other operator would have needed a couple of brawny helpers to pull the truck up and out, but this time the liftman did it alone, as easily as if he were pulling a cork out of a bottle. Then, while Issy and the boys looked on, grinning stupidly, he embraced the fridges one by one and casually deposited them on the floor with a careful, leisurely grace.

'Meet Gary,' Issy said to me. 'King of the *Shleppers*! He's just started this morning.'

Gary was over six feet tall and broad in proportion. He had massive hands, and biceps that swelled through the thin sleeves of his khaki overalls. His face was big and round and friendly, with the splashed nose and thick lips of the negro. His smile was an ad-agent's dream.

He bowed slightly and said, 'How do you do?' Music rippled through his voice.

'What is *shleppers?*' he asked, turning to Issy. The boys laughed at Issy's embarrassment.

'*Shleppers*, Gary,' someone volunteered, 'is the Yid-dish word for porters, carriers, people who have to hump heavy loads.'

'King of the *Shleppers*,' he mused, smiling to himself as he returned to the lift. He was not angry at the title, nor ashamed, nor proud.

He re-entered the lift and I followed him in.

'Where to?' he asked.

'Top, please.'

'Executive floor,' he commented, smiling.

'Not quite, Gary. I'm the new boy in Accounts.'

12

'White-collar, then.' He spoke the words without any trace of envy or heat, almost affectionately. His smile hadn't shifted, the big, snowy teeth like a mouthful of ice cream.

As he opened the lift gate on the sixth floor he turned to me.

'You don't sound London. What part of England you from, man?'

'I'm not from England, Gary. I'm from Ireland.'

'Ireland? Then how come you working for the Jews?'

'That's simple,' I answered. 'I *am* a Jew.'

For the first time the smile vanished – momentarily. Then it blazed back, skittish giggles bubbling from between his huge lips.

'What's the joke?' I asked.

Gary closed the gate behind me and pressed the button. As the lift descended I followed his eyes down with mine. His look was one of childish delight and discovery. 'Man,' he sang, his words dancing with incredulous laughter, 'who ever heard of an Irish Jew?'

I told my parents about Gary when I wrote home that night. He was the first coloured person I had ever met and that was about the most unusual thing that had happened to me in London. But my father wasn't impressed. In his reply – he and my mother took it in turns to write – he said that he didn't see anything funny in Gary's question.

His comment distracted me and made me face myself. For the first time in my life I had been thrown among Jews I hadn't grown up with, Jews I had never met before, and I felt an outsider. That was something my father would never understand. Born in Russia, settled in Ireland – there could hardly be two more different worlds – but all he had done was to move from one small ghetto to another. It was easy for him to believe that all Jews were brothers.

For the rest of the week I didn't exchange more than the odd greeting and smile with Gary. Then, on the Friday, I

13

met him as I was leaving to go home. It was only three o'clock but the November darkness was already closing in, so we were finishing early enough to get home before Sabbath commenced. We filed out the side door, carefully turning our backs as we opened our wage packets, and then casually threw calls of 'Good *Shabbes*', landing them like haloes over each other's head.

Gary was standing in the street, flashing his broad smile and eagerly joining in the exchange of ritual salutation.

'See you in *shul*, Gary,' someone shouted.

'Don't be late, man,' he warned back with mock gravity. As I made to pass him he caught my arm.

'Good *Shabbes*,' he said.

'Thank you, Gary,' I answered. 'Sorry I can't wish you the same.'

'Why not, man?' he rejoined. 'While Ah'm working for this firm, Ah'm an honorary Jew.'

'That's as good as most of us,' cracked Inwards Goods Supervisor Benny Adler.

'You speak for yourself,' I snapped. I hadn't liked Benny since I had sat next to him one lunch hour and found him eating ham sandwiches.

'*Chazar*,' I'd said disgustedly.

'If it's not, I've been done,' Benny had replied, opening a sandwich to confirm it was pig.

'Not the meat,' I'd growled. 'I meant you.'

Benny and the others had taken it as a huge joke. 'Listen to Shamus, boys,' he had shouted. 'Our Irish friend doesn't like pig.' Then in a thick, loud brogue he had turned to me: 'Don't you know that only the best Jews eat pig and the best pigs come from Ireland? I think you're having us on, Shamus. I don't think you're an Irish Jew at all. You're not the one thing or the other, are yah now? Ah, but no hard feelings, Shamus. Here, have a *chazar* sandwich.'

Every day since then Benny had kept the joke going, offering me a ham sandwich and affecting surprise that anyone from the Emerald Isle should disdain such a native dish. The ragging had very quickly grown thin, which is probably why I had been able to take it without getting annoyed, but that Friday, standing out on the already darkening London street, remembering the way the Bride of the Sabbath would be welcomed at home with the reflection of the *Shabbes* candles gleaming in the burnished *Kiddush* cup, the dark, velvety wine bottle resplendent against the snow-white, freshly laundered cloth, the special *Shabbes* dishes arrayed before my parents, and enfolding all, the familiar close embrace of the ancient ritual – ah, I felt, to hell with Benny. I was even going to tell him that he was right – that Gary's claim to be an honorary Jew was not only as good as most of us but better than some, himself for instance. But I didn't. Instead I fell in with the prevailing mood.

'Good *Shabbes*, Gary,' I said with forced humour. 'See you in *shul*.'

I didn't write home that weekend, so I had a bad conscience by the time Monday came round again. It wasn't helped by the conversation – the first one of any length – I had that lunch-hour with Gary.

'You're from Jamaica, Gary,' I said to get the ball rolling.

'Ah was born in Africa,' he answered, 'but my parents went to live in Jamaica when Ah was eight.'

'Oh? That's a bit unusual, isn't it?'

'Well, man, my father is a lawyer, and he figured there was more scope for him in Jamaica.'

What, then, I wondered, was Gary doing in London, operating a lift and sweating his guts out under heavy loads in a Jewish wholesale house?

He took a wallet from his back pocket and extracted a photograph.

'Here,' he said proudly. 'That's my family.'

The picture showed a bearded negro standing stiffly beside a well set up negress. On his other side was a young negro girl, very beautiful. The trio stood on a smooth

15

lawn, and behind them could be seen part of what appeared to be a spacious dwelling house.

'My father and mother and kid sister,' Gary said.

'A fine family, Gary. Distinguished-looking. But how is it you're not following in your father's footsteps?'

Gary smiled. 'You're wrong, man, 'cause that's just what Ah'm doing.'

'How come?'

'Ah go to night school here. Taking my first law examination in the spring.'

'But why here, Gary? Why come all the way to London to work in the day and study at night? Aren't there colleges in Jamaica?'

'Sure there are but, you see, man, Ah think it would be wrong that Ah should study at home and have my father pay for it. Ah wanted to make my own way as soon as possible. Ah just wanted to.'

We talked then about our respective backgrounds and ancestries. And we talked about prejudice. Gary had never himself experienced actual persecution but he had heard from his grandparents the firsthand tales of African slave traders. Just as I had heard from mine, I told him, the firsthand tales of Tsarist *pogroms*. And he was extremely colour-conscious. In the talks we had every lunch-hour for the rest of the week he argued relentlessly and, for him, excitedly about discrimination and the need for those who suffered from it to stick together. Sometimes I was his only audience, sometimes a few of the others would join in. Usually those who did were on his side anyway, so the discussions, though noisy, were peaceful. Which was just as well – his hypersensitivity was trigger-balanced, and no one was anxious to turn a mountain into a volcano. No one, that is, except a complete imbecile – which left the door open for Mr Sam.

Mr Sam and his brother, Mr Abe, were the owners of Levin's. But Mr Abe was the real boss, the brains. Mr Sam was a mere cypher, plug-ugly lucky to be Mr Abe's brother. He was a shrimp of a man who dressed too well and tried to hide his total ineptitude by indulging in the utmost officiousness. But he was careful never to cross his brother's path, and most of his day was spent in the packing department, safely out of harm's way. It was here that, one day, Gary and he joined issue.

The lunch bell had just rung. Gary put his lift on automatic, took up his sandwiches, and made to join me on a bench for the hour. Being white-collar, I hadn't had to wait for the bell and so had got down to the basement early. All the packers had settled to their snacks, but Mr Sam kept opening some goods that had arrived that morning. As Gary passed, Mr Sam stopped him.

'Would you take these pans up to Hardware, please?' he rapped out tersely.

There were dozens of pans to be shifted and Hardware was almost at the top of the building.

Gary did not move but only replied, 'It's lunch-time, Mr Sam. Will Ah get extra time for this when the hour is up?'

Mr Sam's breadcrumb brains were no match for such a situation. Like a dumb animal he could only charge again.

'Will you take these pans up to Hardware, please?' His voice was like a saw.

'But Mr Sam, Ah'm having my lunch. Will I get extra time for this afterwards?'

Conversation quickly trailed off all round us. The tea steamed into the chill air.

'I asked you to take these up to Hardware.' Mr Sam's small eyes glinted, almost striking a reflection from the highly polished pans he was holding.

'And Ah asked you a simple question, Mr Sam. Will Ah get extra time if Ah take them up?'

Mr Sam glared, his ire rising. Gary looked into his eyes and read clearly the message of contempt and outrage. His own eyes held a lifetime's resentment.

Mr Sam had only one answer as his temper burst.

'You're sacked. Take a week's notice.'

'Suits me,' said Gary indifferently, as he ambled to where I was sitting and settled down beside me.

There was a strained silence for some minutes. Mr Sam continued opening parcels but his mind wasn't on the job. And everybody knew what it *was* on. How would he face Mr Abe? A liftman-cum-porter of Gary's prowess and docility was worth his weight in gold. Who the hell was Mr Sam to sack Gary? A month earlier in a similar fit of temper, Mr Sam had sacked the sweeper – an old fellow everyone called 'Bones' – and got away with it, but a decrepit sweeper was just about the only member of the large staff Mr Sam could dare take it on himself to sack.

He edged over towards us.

'Gary, I'd like a word with you.'

'Ah'm having my lunch, Mr Sam.'

Mr Sam had been led down this path once already and he hastily avoided another stalemate.

'You must realize, Gary, that I'm the boss here and it isn't right for you to question my orders.'

Mouths were quickly stuffed with food to stifle the laughter. Mr Sam's tone was sweet reasonableness itself but he was talking balderdash.

Gary lifted his head and with equal reasonableness replied, 'Mr Sam, you gave me a week's notice and Ah accepted. There's no more to be said. Ah'm having my lunch now.'

Mr Sam blundered on, his brother's irate image making him desperate.

'No, no, no, Gary. You must understand.'

But Gary fully understood. He had looked into Mr Sam's eyes and recognized his miserable quarry.

He put down his sandwiches and stood up, towering over his adversary.

'Mr Sam,' he said, in tones noble, righteous, and authoritative, 'you are a very hasty man. And you are also a very ill-bred man. You think that because you have money, and because you are white and Ah'm black, that you can talk to me in any fashion you like. But you do not

18

have that right, Mr Sam. Ah'm not a slave. Ah'm not an animal. And Ah'm not your property. Ah'm six feet of solid, human flesh. You own only my labour, Mr Sam, and you own that only under certain conditions and at certain prescribed times of the day. If you think you have other rights over me, you are mistaken, Mr Sam. And if you think your money or your colour makes you better than me, you are also mistaken, Mr Sam. Ah'm six feet of solid, human flesh, and man for man and brain for brain Ah figure you just don't have any advantage over me at all, Mr Sam.'

'Of course, Gary, of course,' Mr Sam managed to murmur as soon as Gary's flow ceased. 'I did not mean you to think . . . eh, you know . . .'

'That's all right now, Mr Sam. Ah know.'

Mr Sam chose to misunderstand – or maybe he wasn't pretending. 'Yes, Gary, yes. And you can forget that week's notice. Yes?'

'Suits me, Mr Sam. Just so long as you appreciate the relationship between us.'

'Of course, Gary, of course.' A relieved and beaten Mr Sam turned away to go back to his waiting pans.

Gary's speech had fired me with enthusiasm and I was unable to restrain myself.

'Up the Republic!' I whooped, and a cheer arose from the other benches.

Mr Sam whirled round.

'Who said that?' he snapped, and then, as if afraid his question might be answered, he quickly turned tail and hurried out the door with a couple of pans in his hand.

'Up the Republic, up the Republic,' Benny Adler chanted mockingly amid some derisive laughter. 'Shamus, what d'yah mean by these foreign slogans? Up the Republic, bejapers!'

I had had enough of Benny and was still high on the euphoria of Gary's one-man stand.

'Ah, go and shag yourself, Benny,' I said almost carelessly. 'Get lost. Screw yourself.'

19

The boys appreciated this and howled their laughter at Benny. Benny laughed too as he put a hand on my shoulder.

'Shamus,' he said, the brogue thicker than ever, 'I'm surprised at cha. Where didja ever learn such language? Shure it must have been back in the Emerald Isle, I'll be bound,' and without changing his expression he drove his other fist hard into my solar plexus.

I doubled up like an empty sack, gasping for breath, my eyes streaming. It took me almost half a minute to recover and by then Benny Adler had ambled away. I made to lunge after him, murder in my heart. Suddenly Gary's iron arm encircled my chest and plucked me back to his side.

'Easy,' he said, 'cool off. Keep your shirt on.'

'I'll kill the bastard,' I choked. 'Let me go, Gary!'

'Easy, man. Easy. Benny carries too many guns for you. You wouldn't stand a chance. Anyway, how come you want to fight with him? You're brothers, man.'

I stopped struggling and Gary released me. He was right. Benny could have murdered me if I was stupid enough to take him on.

'Brothers!' I ground out savagely, wiping the last of the tears from my eyes. 'With him?'

'Sure,' Gary soothed. 'You're a Jew, aren't you? Well, so is he, man.'

I looked across at Benny Adler. He waved and shouted over to me, 'No hard feelings, Shamus. You're all right – even if you *are* from Oireland. Up the Republic!'

I choked down my anger. It wasn't only on the physical level that I couldn't fight Benny. His blow had knocked the wind out of my body and Gary had knocked it out of my sails. I might not – like the Chinese Jews – look Jewish; I might recoil from my father's ancient, unquestioning allegiances; I might smart at the rebuffs of the prissy Jewish princesses on the upper floors; I might be outraged by Benny's relish of pig meat. But, no matter what, we were all brothers and I was 'all right'.

Who ever heard of an *Irish* Jew, bejapers!

Ancestral Voices

Priests are people, and in the nature of things more likely
to be well-intentioned than not. I want to believe that – I
need to believe it now – though when I was young I believed
the very opposite.

St Dominick's, where I spent all my schooldays, was
staffed solely by priests, and though their humours and
reactions appeared to be the same as those of ordinary
laymen, I still regarded them as a different species. When
one of them stood in front of the class, book or pointer or
chalk in hand, I did not see a man. I saw only a face above
an all-enveloping black cassock that hid every line and
sign of manhood. Ancestral voices had whispered that this
creature was not as other men were, would not think the
thoughts other men think, tell the jokes other men tell, or
want to kiss a girl. Ancestral voices warned that here was a
living symbol of the apostasy that had riven the faith of
my forefathers, Abraham, Isaac, and Jacob, and in the
process had taught the world to despise the Jews. And I
took the warning to heart.

Eddie, my sixteen-year-old son, has no such precon-
ceptions. He's my only son, the youngest of my five children, so he grew up with four sisters and – until my wife
passed away a few years ago – five mothers. That used to
worry me. I was afraid they'd make him soft and intro-
verted – the sort of youngster I was, though for very different reasons. But Eddie isn't a bit like that. He's a
confident, athletic, normal boy – I believe 'laid back' is the
term used nowadays. And he isn't afraid of priests. On the

contrary: it seems that his prowess at games so impressed Father Patrick, the school coach, that the priest devised a special training schedule for him which he personally supervises. Eddie never misses a session; he refers to the priest as 'Pat'.

I had never given much thought to their friendship. Indeed, I was rather pleased about it, especially when it brought back the recollection of how I had behaved on the only occasion a priest had offered *me* friendship. That was a very long time ago but I still can't blame myself. We may shape our own ends, but we have no control over our beginnings.

It happened on a hot summer afternoon during the school holidays. Early in the morning I had gone out to Bray, a little seaside resort near Dublin, taking sandwiches, a flask of milk and a book, and had spent hours lazing in the sun, daydreaming and reading. Up high on Bray Head – it was midweek and there wasn't anyone to disturb me – had been the perfect spot to enjoy the sort of blissful, solitary withdrawal I rather wallowed in at the time, and later, as I sat in the deserted railway station waiting for the train back to the city, I was still immersed in my book.

'I think the train must be a bit late.'

Those were the first words Father Damien spoke.

I looked up, startled to hear a voice address me, and even more startled by the person it came from. Towering over me was this tall howitzer shape, all coal-coloured and dark with the sun inked out behind his black hat and the clerical collar almost hidden under a strong, shadowed chin.

'No,' I replied, timidly disagreeing, 'it's not due for a while.'

'Ah, that explains why it isn't even in the station yet. I thought for sure it'd be ready and waiting.'

This time I didn't reply – I was too busy listening to my ancestral voices.

Of course in those days I was virtually in thrall to them.

As I grew up I dropped my religious inhibitions one by one and the voices gradually fell silent, so that by the time I met Eddie's friend, Father Pat, I thought I had done with them for ever. It was Miriam, my youngest daughter, who started them off again.

Miriam, nineteen, is always urging me to 'get with it'. Ada and Ray, my two eldest, are both married, and Beth, the studious one, is completely absorbed by her post-graduate research. So it's left to Miriam to keep me on my toes. I know what she means when she says I should 'get with it'. She doesn't actually expect me to *do* anything about changing my habits – not at my age – but she tells me that my attitude is 'antediluvian'. What I dismiss as obnoxious fads and fancies are here to stay, she says; they're accepted and enjoyed everywhere – 'even behind the Iron Curtain', as if that shows how thoroughly obstinate I am in condemning them. God knows I don't believe the world I grew up in was anywhere near perfect, but at least it had standards and you knew where you were with it. Father Pat was a case in point.

The night he came to the house, he was wearing a T-shirt and jeans. The 'mod' get-up completely threw me. Indeed, if it hadn't been for his advancing baldness I could almost have taken him and Eddie to be classmates! I don't think I'd have been at all ill-at-ease if he had been dressed like a normal priest, though paradoxically it had been the opposite when I was confronted by Father Damien. In *his* case it was the sight of the cloth that alarmed me – that and the quiet smile so full of presumption. There was no mistaking its invitation to move up and make room for him, even though there was plenty of room on either side of where I sat in the middle of the bench.

Of course I moved – priests weren't argued with or defied in those days, certainly not by the young, and least of all by a Jewish schoolboy. But this Jewish schoolboy had his ancestral voices to contend with, so in an effort to discourage further conversation I moved right to the extreme edge of the seat and buried my head back in my book. I see now how churlish my behaviour was; I can only hope that Father Damien put it down to shyness.

Perhaps Father Pat, too, made the same allowance for my awkward manner that first night we met. He had called for Eddie on the way to a tactics talk about some important match or other they were having the next day, and Eddie insisted he come in and meet the family.

'This is my dad, Pat,' he said, 'and my sister, Miriam.'

We shook hands, I stumbling over calling him 'Father'. I hadn't expected that Eddie would address him as 'Pat' in company and I had a confused feeling that my being so conventional was stamping me as a fuddy-duddy. Miriam called out her usual breezy 'Hi' and the priest echoed it back, raising a brisk, open-handed salute, Red Indian-style. I fetched a couple of beers – Eddie had a soft drink – and we all chatted sociably.

That was the first conversation of any length I had had with a priest since my meeting with Father Damien. But what a difference between the two encounters! With Pat, I was the host, Eddie's father, which put me in the position of having to be friendly; with Father Damien I was intent on keeping myself to myself. The thing about priests, however – Irish priests, anyway – is that they are trained to be outgoing and patient, so I found it wasn't that easy to rebuff Father Damien.

'Which one are you reading?' he asked as soon as he was seated.

I looked at him vacantly, noticing the soft blue eyes behind the heavy spectacles.

'Which one? Which poem?'

He had seen the name Yeats on the cover of my book. I made an involuntary move to put my hand over it but he pretended not to notice, easing my embarrassment by not waiting for an answer.

'Do you read a lot of poetry?'

I mumbled something that must have been unintelligible.

'Ah yes,' he replied, lifting his voice at the end to cut off my retreat.

Even now, recollection of that moment of panic makes me go cold. Never before had I felt so trapped. I had spent all my youth grazing inside my ancestral stockade, protected from any close contact with outsiders. Now here I was, fully exposed to one of those outsiders – and a priest moreover.

'I used to read a lot of poetry when I was your age,' he said half to himself. There was a sadness in his voice and he looked straight ahead as he spoke, almost as if he was looking back towards some lost paradise. I was lulled into a response.

'Did – did you read Yeats?'

'I did indeed. Do you know his poem "Sailing to Byzantium"?

> *An aged man is but a paltry thing,*
> *A tattered coat upon a stick, unless*
> *Soul clap its hands and sing . . .*

That was my favourite. That line, *unless/Soul clap its hands and sing . . .* It's such an exciting image. There's something mystical about it – the corporeal and the incorporeal all in one. Take a beautiful day like today: wouldn't it just make your soul clap its hands and sing?'

Hearing the priest praise that line increased my unease. I knew souls were important to Catholics, but I had never heard any talk of them at home. I didn't even know if I had one. And mixed in with my fear of the subject was embarrassment at my ignorance.

I was embarrassed by my ignorance when talking to Father Pat, too. Not that he said anything about the soul. Rugby, something particularly corporeal to judge from the bruises Eddie sometimes came home with, was his enthusiasm. I had never taken any interest in the game, so when Father Pat put his arm around Eddie's neck in a comradely hug, saying, 'This young man will be a star one day. Take it from me – he'll play for Ireland yet,' perhaps it was shame rather than embarrassment I felt at my ignorance of my son's promise. Eddie blushed at the compliment and slapped his friend's hand in mock chastisement.

'Wouldn't you come along yourself tomorrow and see him play?' Father Pat suggested.

I said that perhaps it might put Eddie off if he knew I was there watching him. Eddie didn't contradict me, but the priest persisted. 'You could come with Eddie. Or if that's too early for you, ask for me at the gate when you arrive and I'll collect you. You'll have the best seat in the park – right next to me on the coach's bench.'

'That's very good of you,' I smiled, but I didn't intend to accept his offer. If Eddie had asked me to go to the game, I'm sure I would have agreed, but I wouldn't have wanted any special privileges from Father Pat. Perhaps subconsciously I was remembering what the special privilege Father Damien had forced on me that day in the railway station had led to.

Immediately the train we had been waiting for arrived, a fat porter, his cap back on his head and a red handkerchief tied around his neck, scuttled to the exit to take the tickets from the few people who alighted. It was not a long train, and as the passengers disappeared there was hardly anybody left in it. I moved towards the third-class carriages in the rear, while Father Damien made to cross my path towards the first-class section. As I drew back and prepared to smile him away, he placed an arm around my shoulders and steered me along beside him.

'There's an empty carriage here,' he said.

It happened so unexpectedly, so swiftly, that I had no time to do anything about it. Docilely I stepped into the carriage, protesting that I didn't have a first-class ticket, but Father Damien directed me into a corner seat and settled himself back opposite me, saying, 'Sure that needn't worry you.' Then he leaned across and gave my knee a comforting squeeze.

The first half of the journey that followed must have been something of a nightmare to me. I could think of nothing except how I would explain to the ticket collector my presence in a first-class carriage when all I had was a third-class ticket. My memory presents a jumble of green fields, cows and cottages seen through the carriage window, interspersed by sleepy stations that the train barely disturbed in its halting passage. Of Father Damien's conversation at that stage, or of my part in it, nothing remains.

But I needn't have worried. When the carriage door was opened and the collector appeared, calling 'Tickets, please', the priest smoothly took mine from my reluctantly outstretched hand and gave it up with his. Even as the collector's eyebrows rose and his mouth opened to challenge me, Father Damien said quickly, 'That's all right – the boy's with me.' The reaction was instantaneous: a soft grunt of obeisance, an ingratiating smile, a touch of the cap – and the collector was gone.

I should have felt relief. I did, but only for a few moments, for soon Father Damien had started to chatter again.

'What parish are you from?'

I hesitated, confused. 'I don't know. I mean I don't know its name.'

'Ah!'

His exclamation sounded self-satisfied, as if my answer had confirmed some suspicion in his mind.

He knows you're a Jew, the ancestral voices warned. *Be careful.* But what was it I had to be careful of? No one had ever really explained.

'Where do you go to school?' he asked.

I told him. He nodded and commended the school's record.

'I suppose you'll be one of their Scholarship prospects?'

I blushed – it was the kind of flattery that forced a blush – but I was more annoyed than embarrassed. Left-handed compliments based on assumed racial aptitudes were just as unthinking as would have been left-handed sneers based on assumed racial stigmas.

'Do you get on well with the boys in your class, you do?'

I said I did.

'I suppose you're friends with some of them. Special friends, I mean,' he added when I appeared uncomprehending.

'Not special.'

'Perhaps you prefer the girls,' he added with a crooked smile.

I reddened. 'I don't know any girls. Except my sisters.'

'How many sisters have you?'

'Four.'

'That's a coincidence,' Father Damien said. 'I have four sisters myself.'

He turned his head away and fell silent for a while. Then he began to talk again, drawing my attention to a copse of elm trees that the train was passing. They reminded him of the Abbey, the place where he lived with many other priests. He went on to tell me about it and about his life there. Detail by detail he built up a picture of warmth and peace and dedication. But there were moments when his voice trailed off, and in those silences he would look away from the window and turn his eyes on me. I felt uncomfortable under his soft stare, but took refuge in the knowledge that Dublin and release were only a mile or two away.

He was still talking when the train reached its destination, and as he grew purposeful again, I found I was being assured how much I would like the Abbey if I cared to visit it. Caught off guard, anxious only to escape, I nodded politely.

'Then how about next Tuesday? Can you manage that?'

Once again I was too slow, too taken by surprise, and my hesitation was sufficient to give him the wrong impression.

'Great,' he said as we stood outside the busy station, with the homegoing travellers hurrying past us between the massive, grimy pillars, and the swaying trams clanging along the road. 'I'll pick you up here at seven-thirty on Tuesday.' Stooping a little to shake my hand, he murmured, almost confidentially, 'We can have more time together then,' before turning to disappear into the crowd.

I cursed my timidity, my reluctance to speak up for

myself. Or was it an ingrained deference towards a member of the clergy? I suppose it could have been, for I nearly caused the same sort of misunderstanding with Father Pat when I didn't immediately decline his first invitation to the rugby match. Fortunately, however, that time I was given a second chance. As he was leaving with Eddie, he said, 'I'll see you tomorrow, will I?' and I was able to reply, 'I'll do my best. But don't rely on it.'

I doubt that he was disappointed when I didn't turn up. Anyway, in the euphoria of winning the match – for win it they did – he'd hardly have thought any the worse of me. But what had Father Damien thought as he waited for me that Tuesday evening, waited unavailingly?

After we had parted on the station steps, I stood in a trance, horrified. Why should he want to see me again? What unimaginable danger had I let myself in for? I had no idea, but fear made me decide there and then not to find out, and my ancestral voices provided all the approbation I needed. In the next few days visions of Father Damien pacing up and down outside the station at seven-thirty on Tuesday evening troubled my conscience, but once Tuesday had passed I quickly forgot all about our meeting.

No doubt I would have forgotten all about my meeting with Father Pat, too, were it not for Miriam.

'What did you think of him?' she asked after I had seen him and Eddie to the front door and wished them luck for the match.

'He seems all right,' I said. 'A nice enough man. Not what I'd have expected a priest to look like. But then these days . . .'

'He's as queer as a coot, of course,' Miriam said, quite conversationally.

'Queer? How do you mean?'

She turned to me, a pained expression on her face.

'Oh, Daddy! Where *have* you have been all these years! He's gay – as gay as they come. Surely you must have noticed.'

I looked at Miriam with amazement. I hadn't noticed. I never do notice these things. They had never been part of the world I knew. Discos, drugs, sex, gays – they were the world of Miriam's generation.

'Are you sure?' I asked.

'Of course I'm sure. A blind man could see it.'

No, my daughter, a blind man couldn't see it. A blind man sees nothing. Like your father. What else hadn't I seen? Because it suddenly hit me, hit me hard and cold in my gut, and my heart gave a lurch: if Father Pat was gay, was Eddie too?

I could have asked Miriam, she was so knowing. But would I believe her if she told me he wasn't? Homosexuality probably didn't upset her, but she could have no doubt about the effect it would have on me if I knew that my own son was . . . queer. I began to think about the strangeness of Eddie's friendship with Father Pat – a Catholic priest and a Jewish youth. I began to read the worst into the way Father Pat had put an arm around Eddie's shoulders, into the embarrassed, almost dainty slap Eddie had given him. I was appalled. Could it possibly be? The newspapers were full of talk about homosexuality. More and more people were admitting openly to it. And priests were people too.

Then they started – the ancestral voices. After all those years they had come to life again and brought back with them what I had buried half a century before: the memory of Father Damien. Chilling and stark it bloomed in my mind, as if the rubble of the years between had merely served to keep it fresh and intact until something should happen to uncover it. Once more I was back in that carriage, feeling the grip of his hand on my knee, the hunger of his eyes on my face. Had he, too, been . . .?

I sat alone for a long time that night, trying to sort out my thoughts. All my inadequacies pressed in on me, all my failings – as a person and as a father. I told myself that even if Miriam had been right about Father Pat, that was no reason to suspect Eddie. I had nothing to go on, just as so long ago I had had no reason whatever to reject Father Damien – apart from those damned ancestral voices. So Eddie had a friendship with a priest. So what? If I hadn't listened to those voices, I, too, might have had such a friendship.

I was completely exhausted by the time I fell into bed. Appalled, too, at the prospect of questioning Eddie. Surely that sort of man-to-man talk between father and son was hopelessly out of date. Boys these days learned everything about sex very early – how could they not? It was all around them.

Next morning brought me some relief when I remembered it was the day of his big match and so there could be no question of confronting him just then. And when his team won, the next few days never seemed to offer the right opportunity. So in the end I did ask Miriam.

She's a cool one, that girl. I thought the question would shock her, at the very least surprise her. But she took it in her stride. Hardly glancing up from her magazine, she shrugged her shoulders and said, 'I don't know. It never struck me. I never thought about it.'

'Do you mean', I pursued hesitantly, 'that it never struck you he might be . . . or that you never thought about it at all?'

'Never thought about it at all really.'

'Think about it now, Miriam.'

She put her magazine aside and thought about it. For a whole second. Then she gave her verdict.

'I mean, we don't see a great deal of Eddie, do we, so it's hard to tell. Besides, when you live with someone, you don't notice some things. Same with your friends. I mean, ten per cent of the male population is supposed to be gay, so how many of your own friends are, without you knowing. You could be one of the ten per cent yourself and *they* needn't know, need they?'

'Miriam!'

She laughed. 'Joke, Dad, only a joke.'

She said no more. Neither did I. It was obvious that

Miriam couldn't, or wouldn't, help me. Something told me too that she would make sure of getting to Eddie before I did and forewarning him. How ironic! With Father Damien it was ancestral voices that had kept me in ignorance – now my own children were doing the same.

Is there a lesson for me somewhere in all this?

Mr Kyak and the Coming of the Messiah

It was almost too much of a coincidence – J.D. coming in just after a large piece had broken off one of my teeth. He visited us very seldom and I had never once been inside his surgery – yet now here he was, out of the blue, apologizing for interrupting our supper while I was running my tongue over the jagged tooth that made me, so unexpectedly, his prospective patient. The suddenness of the catastrophe was such that I would have bared my mouth to him immediately were it not obvious that he had news to tell. He informed us that Mr Kyak had just died.

'Poor soul,' my mother lamented. She made the loss seem personal, though Mr Kyak had been a very solitary and inconspicuous member of our community. Really we knew him only to salute.

'When?' enquired my father.

'About an hour ago.' J.D.'s mouth twitched in one corner and his parchment-coloured skin was as white as if *he* were the corpse. J.D. was secretary of the Burial Society, a most efficient secretary, a carrier of bad news second to none. His voice dropped, creating a respectful silence. For a moment my tongue paused over my broken tooth while I tried to think of Mr Kyak dead. But death was still unknown to me and remote, as little known and remote as Mr Kyak had been, whereas my broken tooth was a personal horror, abrupt, immediate, foundation-shaking. My tongue probed on.

'The funeral is tomorrow . . . twelve o'clock,' J.D. announced.

'Twelve o'clock,' my father grunted. 'Have you fixed up the cars?'

'We'll have plenty. Myer and Abram, Jack Caplan, Issy . . . we won't be short.'

'A cup of tea, Mr Kirsch?' my mother suggested.

'No, thank you.' J.D.'s parchment cracked into an automatic smile but his mind was elsewhere. Still, the offer was enough to remind him that he hadn't taken his hat off. Like a man brushing flies from his bald pate he swept it off now, revealing his crumpled *yarmulkah*, and darted a look at me. For some reason I guiltily stopped probing at my tooth.

'Who's with him now?' my father asked, bringing my thoughts back to Mr Kyak.

'Cecil.'

'Who else?'

'No one yet. I thought you might go.' J.D. made the suggestion reluctantly. He was always afraid his suggestions would be ridiculed – which they usually were.

'To stay all night? *He* can go.' My father jerked his head in my direction. Once again my tongue was stilled over my tooth.

J.D. wouldn't have minded who stayed with the corpse once Cecil Jacobs had a companion for the night vigil. But I had never watched before – I wasn't even a member of the Burial Society. So J.D. hesitated, pecking in doubt, all the lines on his skin frowning separately.

'He's old enough to start,' my father commented in a dry tone.

'But he's not a member of the Society.'

'I can assure you Mr Kyak won't mind that.'

I gave an involuntary laugh at my father's gallows humour and then immediately regretted it. It made J.D. think I was willing. But I wasn't. I had never seen death before and I had a sudden fear of seeing it now.

'Finish your supper first,' J.D. said quickly, 'and then we'll go.'

'I'm finished,' I muttered. How could they expect me

to eat supper before going to sit with a corpse?

'You haven't started it yet,' my father pointed out.

'Well, I can't eat any more with my broken tooth.' It was a good excuse for my sudden loss of appetite.

'Let Mr Kirsch see it.'

'Did you break your tooth?' J.D. asked, so unemotionally that I felt slighted.

'*I* didn't break it! It just broke off on its own.'

J.D. stood over me and peered into my mouth. He twisted my head around to the light.

'It's nothing serious,' he said, sitting down again. 'Just rotten in the middle.'

'Rotten?' I echoed in amazement.

'Right through.'

'But I never knew! I haven't had a bad tooth in all my life! It never even pained me!'

'Doesn't have to. I'll fill that easily. Come up to me after the funeral.'

I shook my head, mesmerized at the realization that I had a tooth rotten right through and never even knew it.

'Well, if you're ready, we'll go,' J.D. suggested.

I got up silently, my tongue chiding at the rotten tooth, my mind appalled as if at some sort of betrayal.

The death house was in a quiet street – a small house made gloomy and foreboding by the half-drawn blinds. J.D. did not knock on the front door but opened it by pulling a string latched inside the letter-box. He led me into the hall, dark and narrow, and up a steep flight of stairs. Almost each step creaked, and the noise made me notice the house's silence.

Reaching the landing, J.D. knocked lightly on one of the doors.

'I think this is the room,' he said.

We heard a quick, heavy tread and the door was flung open by Cecil Jacobs. He was a middle-aged man, a lusty widower, with a stomach of fine protuberance, but his hearty greeting died when he saw me.

'It's all right, we'll elect him at the next meeting,' J.D. assured him testily, anxious as usual to forestall criticism.

'Bugger that,' was the answer.

'He'll be all right,' J.D. repeated. 'There's nothing to it. He's got to start some time.'

I followed J.D. into the room and shut the door. Immediately I noticed the dry, choking smell. I supposed it to be the smell of death. J.D. and Cecil Jacobs had moved over to the other side of the room where I sensed, rather than saw, a bed on which I sensed, rather than saw, the remains of Mr Kyak.

I sat down on an empty chair, afraid to look, but telling myself that it would be all right to look, that there was nothing to see. So I looked. J.D. and Cecil Jacobs were standing by the side of the bed, their backs to me, gazing down at the corpse of Mr Kyak. Most of his body was hidden by them, but not his head. It was on his head that my gaze fastened. I had taken for granted a sheet covering everything away, but there was no sheet. Just the bare visage, the colour of paste, looking colder than marble, and utterly lifeless. The shock struck me numb and made me forget to breathe.

The phrase 'He fell asleep . . .' rushed to mind. I could understand now how tempting such a phrase was. If one did not look, but only said often enough, 'He fell asleep . . .', the blow might be softened. Not for me, however, just then. I did not seek a phrase which would make death seem like life; I wanted it made different, set completely apart, so I would not be reminded of it. But, looking on Mr Kyak, he appeared indeed only to have fallen asleep, and I was horrified by the resemblance. I started to tremble, then stopped almost immediately when my ears suddenly began to hear again the voices of J.D. and Cecil Jacobs and I became aware that they were talking about me. I was curious to know what they were saying, but something was preventing me from concentrating on their words and forcing me to keep my gaze on Mr Kyak's dead face. I felt in some deep, obscure way unwell.

J.D. and Cecil Jacobs turned round. Both of them pinned me with probing, unhappy looks and J.D. raised his hat for a moment to wipe his forehead. The atmosphere was becoming unbearably heavy. Though the two windows in the room were open at the top, the half-drawn blinds were keeping the smell in and the fresh air out. I loosened my collar.

'Hurry up and get the candles anyway,' Cecil Jacobs was saying.

'I won't be very long,' J.D. replied as he left the room.

Cecil Jacobs continued to stand in the same position, his hat tilted back on his head, his hands clasped behind him so that his belly was urged forward. I could sense his unease.

'Why don't you sit on the other chair?' he suddenly asked me. 'Go on, it's more comfortable.'

'No, not at all, Mr Jacobs,' I gabbled back. 'You sit there. I don't mind the hard chair.'

He continued to look at me for a moment, then shrugged his belly, and reluctantly moved away from the bed. For the first time since I had entered the room, Mr Kyak's body, from the neck down, was revealed to me. It had on only a short cotton pyjama coat that reached hardly as far as the thin buttocks, and even from where I was sitting I could see there was something wrong with the part that was uncovered.

Cecil Jacobs stopped half-way to his chair.

'Take a proper look,' he said. 'Then you can forget it.'

He turned and moved back to the bed. Drawn as if by a magnet, I stood up and joined him beside the corpse. I took a proper look. Mr Kyak's genitals – what had been Mr Kyak's genitals – were now a horrible blue mess, swollen, oozing, and putrid. It was from them that the awful stench was rising. I made no sound at the sight, but a scream shot through me like a rocket, up from my own genitals, up through my frozen body, and out through the hole in my rotten tooth to split into a million sparks in my head. I must have reeled away, for Cecil Jacobs grabbed me by the arm and humped me back to the chair.

'Take it with a laugh, man!' he urged. 'Take it with a laugh! No need to let it get you down.'

I don't remember being actually placed in the chair by him, nor do I remember seeing where he brought the bottle of whiskey from, but the next thing I knew was that a glass was in my hand and he was pushing it to my lips.

'Drink it down! That's the right stuff for this business. Right down with it!'

I threw my head back and gulped, too paralysed to be prepared for the kick. It was as if another rocket had been fired off inside me – only this time on the return journey – starting in my head, flashing down through my rotten tooth, and exploding like a burning fountain in my belly.

I gave a long breath and squeezed the tears out of my eyes. The room was a blur, my head was throbbing, and my tooth was giving me hell.

'Feeling better?' Cecil Jacobs asked.

'No. Awful,' I groaned.

'Ah, what's the matter with you? Take these things with a laugh! If that's the worst sight you'll see in your life, you're a lucky man.'

'It's not that,' I replied hastily, not wanting him to know how sick with shock I was.

'What is it then?'

'It's my tooth.'

'Your tooth? What's wrong with it?'

'It broke earlier. It's rotten right through. J.D. is going to fill it tomorrow.'

'Let's see.'

I opened my mouth and Cecil Jacobs pushed his face so close that I could smell the whiskey on his breath.

'Ah yes, I see. Black as the Ace of Spades. Have you bad teeth?'

'No,' I denied. 'I never had a toothache in my life. This happened suddenly. I had no idea it was bad.'

'You probably have a lot more. There's always more than one bad. Is it still paining you?'

'Yes.'

'Here – have some more whiskey. Best thing for a toothache. Don't swallow it quickly – just keep it against the tooth.'

He had it poured out before I could stop him so I put the glass to my lips and allowed a little of the drink to drain against the tooth. I sat there, my jaw bulging slightly, my head ringing, and looked again at Mr Kyak.

'What did he die of?' I asked, almost gargling the whiskey in my cheek.

'You saw for yourself,' Cecil Jacobs replied, putting the bottle to his lips. Seeing him swallow, I involuntarily swallowed also. This time the effect was more pleasurable, so I took another mouthful of whiskey and held it against my tooth.

Cecil Jacobs' answer hadn't told me anything, and the fascination of Mr Kyak's rancid genitals urged me on.

'But how did it happen? What caused it?'

'Too much of what you fancy,' Cecil Jacobs answered, and his belly bounced with mirth.

The idea of Mr Kyak meeting with such an end was too ludicrous and I began to laugh also. The activity made me swallow my last mouthful of whiskey but Cecil Jacobs quickly poured me some more. My whole face was on fire now, not only my tooth, and the atmosphere of the room was like a plague.

'No, really, what *did* cause such a mess?'

'I dunno. Some disease or other. Some germ, it must be.'

'A germ? But couldn't they cure it?'

'Evidently not. I suppose no one knows it's there until it's too late and the rotting has started.'

'And it killed him in the end,' I said, drinking the whiskey now without bothering to rest it against my tooth.

'So it seems,' Cecil Jacobs agreed. 'He's dead, anyway.'

He laughed as if he had made a joke.

'It gets us all in the long run,' he said, 'one way or

another. But there's no use worrying about it. You've got to take it with a laugh.'

I could hear Cecil Jacobs' voice fill the room but I wasn't really listening to it. I sat drinking the whiskey and gazing at Mr Kyak's genitals.

'It got him in the end,' I mused.

Cecil Jacobs poured me some more whiskey.

'It got him in the beginning,' I half-shouted suddenly. 'Once it started, he was gone. Once the germ started, he was rotting from that moment.'

'So what? Worrying about it won't help. When your number's up, lad, there's nothing you can do.'

Cecil Jacobs drank down his whiskey and poured himself some more. My tongue began to probe again at my rotten tooth, my face felt like a hot balloon, and the horrible smell in the room made me imagine that I was beginning to rise up and float. I looked at Mr Kyak and thought of the germ he had known nothing about until it had been too late. He had been rotting away all the time . . .

I jumped up so suddenly that the remains of my drink splashed on to the floor.

'I think I'm going to be sick.'

'What's wrong? What is it?' Cecil Jacobs started to his feet and caught my arm. 'Is it your tooth?'

'No,' was all I could say before I felt too dizzy to continue standing. I plonked back in the chair and held my head in my hands.

'Go on, be sick. Best thing,' Cecil Jacobs urged. 'I'll find the lavatory for you.'

'No,' I groaned, too bad to move. I sat for a while until the dizziness passed and I felt a little better.

Just then J.D. returned, carrying some large candles. He had brought Jack Caplan with him.

J.D. took a look at me and said to Cecil Jacobs, 'What happened to him?'

'How do I know?' Cecil Jacobs barked back. 'You said he'd be all right.'

'His father told me to take him,' J.D. protested. 'It's not my fault.'

Jack Caplan lifted me by the arm.

'I'll take him home.'

'Best thing,' Cecil Jacobs grunted. 'But you'll come back?'

'Yes, I'll be back in ten minutes.'

I allowed Jack Caplan to guide me down the stairs, making a lot of noise as he prevented me from falling.

'Ssh,' he whispered.

'Yes,' I agreed. 'Ssh. Mr Kyak'sh dead.'

He opened the front door and led me to his car. I stood waiting for him to get out his keys. The air seemed to be made of light, strong breezes that lifted me off the ground and tickled my nose. I giggled at Jack Caplan searching for his keys.

'What's wrong with you?' he said.

I laughed back at him, loudly this time.

'Shut up, you fool, and get in,' he hissed.

I thought it was a good joke, Jack Caplan being angry with me, and I got into the car, laughing even more.

'How much whiskey did you have up there?' he asked as he drove off. 'I think you're drunk.'

That was even funnier still and I began to laugh my head off.

'Tell me the joke,' he said.

I couldn't tell him I was laughing at what he said, so I told him something else.

'I broke my tooth. Want to see it?'

I pushed my face up to his.

'Not now, you fool,' he barked. 'I'm trying to drive.'

I was still laughing and at the same time trying to probe my rotten tooth with my tongue. I couldn't do both together, and the more I tried, the more I laughed.

Jack Caplan was glad when he got me home.

'Shall I go in with you?'

'No,' I said, beginning to float away from him. 'Mr Kyak'sh waiting for you.'

He was laughing himself as he drove off.

I wandered up the stairs and into my room. My bed slid up to meet me and I fell on to it. Pulling myself up, I took off my clothes, but when I tried to put on my pyjamas I found myself still fully dressed. Carefully, laughing quietly, I undressed again until I stood naked. Then I put on my pyjama coat and searched for the trousers. Wherever I had dropped them, I couldn't find them now. The more I searched, the more I couldn't find them. It was ridiculous. I lay on the bed in only the pyjama coat, and then I remembered. Of course, poor Mr Kyak had no pyjama trousers so he must have borrowed mine.

I fell asleep wondering how long it might be before I'd get them back. Perhaps not until the Day of Judgement, when the Messiah would send Leviathan throughout all the seven seas to collect the bodies and souls of the Jews for their journey to Paradise. Mr Kyak would be sitting on its snout, my pyjama trousers decently covering his now-restored genitals, and I would join him, my full set of healthy teeth answering his happy grin. It was the most vivid dream I had ever had, and as the fabulous fish carried us nearer and nearer to God, I was crying with joy.

When I woke in the morning my pillow was wet with tears. But the joy in my heart did not last. It was quickly transformed by an unutterable sorrow when I remembered that this was the day Mr Kyak was going to be put under the ground and I was going to have my rotten tooth filled. 'Take it with a laugh,' Cecil Jacobs had counselled! The only thing I could find to laugh at was the idea that sometime, many millennia in the future, there would come a day when Mr Kyak and I, made whole again, would sail through the gates of Heaven on the back of a huge, friendly whale.

Monty's Monday

In spinning for Monty Levinson's destiny – and this is how Monty himself looked at it – the slot machine of Fate had come up with three lemons: it had made him a Jew in a small community – in Waterford, a small town – in Ireland, a small country. Actually, had the machine been geared for a fourth symbol, that would have been another lemon, for if it had been Monty's luck to be born at the turn of the nineteenth century instead of half-way through the twentieth, he might not have found himself so at odds with his times. But, as it was, the three lemons he had identified gave him quite enough to be sucking on throughout his teenage years, especially as they had some hard-to-swallow pips in them too. Pip one: he was the youngest of four brothers. Pip two: the other three were all brainy and he wasn't. Pip three: they were ambitious and had graduated from university (two doctors, one dentist), while *his* only aim in life was to avoid work. Pip four: they were now practising in London, no doubt with delectable dolls on tap, while he was stuck in Waterford, reduced to half-heartedly wooing the far-from-exciting community heiress, Myra Rhinegold. And pip five, the one that really stuck in his craw: their desertion (as he saw it) meant that the responsibility of carrying on the family fancy goods business fell completely on him.

If he didn't actually hate what he was doing (except on Monday mornings), he was certainly thoroughly browned off with it. But he had been trapped, hadn't he? Trapped by his brothers one after another dashing their father's hopes that they would go into the business. So what that they had afforded their parents the coveted *yiches* that came from going to a university and acquiring initials after their names? Easy for them to take such a course when, apart from having the necessary brains and *zitzfleisch*, each one knew that there was always another mug behind him to release him from his filial obligations. Last one in bed puts out the light! So Monty, the hind-tit, would have to fulfil their father's hopes of having a son in the business; *his* father, of blessed memory, had started the very first day he arrived from Poland, a penniless refugee. Year after year that bearded man had tramped through the villages of southern Ireland, knocking on every door, a pack on his back, a bulging suitcase in each hand, and his *Siddur* and holy phylacteries in his pocket. His son, Solomon, Monty's father, had followed in his footsteps – literally. And in the fullness of time Solomon Levinson had prospered, was able to marry, raise a family, put three boys through university. It was an achievement, something to be proud of, to hold on to. Solomon Levinson would not see it all abandoned. Surely out of four sons one could be found to follow in *his* footsteps? It wasn't as if they were being asked to hump packs like a donkey, as he had done. No, no, the business could afford a car now.

So it came to pass that on Monty had been heaped all his accumulated disappointment, all his mounting frantic hopes. And, fortunately for him, Monty had nowhere else to turn. Not that there weren't other places, other countries that beckoned: England, America, Israel even! And the times were right too: the Swinging Sixties! Everywhere – so the newspapers and magazines assured him – youth was having its fling. But Monty stayed put, chafing, feeling hard done by, telling himself that family loyalty alone stopped him from leaving, not recognizing that he didn't want to leave, that he only wanted to want to. Solomon, overjoyed, did all he could to mollify him – and to tie the knot tighter. He changed the name of the business from Levinson's to S. Levinson & Son, and had fancy cards printed proclaiming Monty to be their 'Representative'. The effect on Monty's self-image was minimal; as far as he was concerned, he was still the traditional *viklanik*, the weekly payments man, not much more than a motorized version of the age-old Wandering Jew.

The pin-pricks of his enforced occupation were many and they started right at the beginning of the working week with the Monday-morning feeling. Monday morning was welcomed by him no less sulkily than it was by any other young man forced to rise early and flog himself back into a labouring groove after a hard weekend of pleasure. And for Monty the recurring torture was more purgatorial than for those not correspondingly situated, since they never experienced the disorientation of being regularly uprooted from the comforts of home to be deposited, headachy and bloodshot-eyed, automatic smile and false *bonhomie* turned to full voltage, among a world of temporarily foreign natives.

Yet on this particular Monday morning, Monty, though tasting life bitterer than ever, was desperately eager to be off. While loading samples into his car he was straining so much at the leash that eventually even old Solomon noticed it, and, grateful that his son was at last showing signs of appreciating his good fortune, the old man offered up a silent prayer of gratitude to the Lord, blessed and be blessed His Holy Name.

Monty, however, was feeling anything but benedictive, and had he known of his father's prayer he would probably have asked the Lord to transfer it to a more worthwhile credit than that for which it had been offered. There was nothing about the fancy goods business of Solomon Levinson & Son that attracted him on this Monday morning more particularly than on any other, nor had he developed a sudden solicitude for its many customers scattered over a succession of small towns and villages throughout central and southern Ireland. Nor – since this was the only other present and external circumstance which might conceivably have motivated his impatience – was it the weather, hot though it was, that had induced in Monty such a rare nervous flap over a Monday morning.

But if it was none of these attractions that made Monty jog his father through his final wheezed instructions and silently mutter to himself a clipped 'Thank God that's over' as he at last started up the engine and commenced his journey, then what was it? The answer was simple: people – and the frenetic need to escape from their orbit. Not just the ordinary, common or garden inoffensive man or woman in the street, but Monty's brethren, the Jewish folk of Waterford, that severely attenuated and constantly shrinking community set in an oasis of alien surroundings (as any wandering Jewish chronicler always got around, one way or another, to putting it) and very particularly its foremost female prize – Myra, the fattening, inheritance-laden daughter of Jacob (Diamond Jim) Rhinegold.

As Monty honked his way through the clogged traffic towards the bright freedom of the country roads, he reflected grimly that his previous night's caper with Myra had effectively administered a sharp set-back to his campaign as leading suitor for her hand and hundreds – and if she carried out her threat to report the same caper to her father, matters might not end there. Deep down he did not really believe that his prospects had been permanently damaged, but that did nothing to alleviate his distress. Being the type who took all small annoyances greatly to heart while remaining paralytically calm in the face of major disasters, he was constantly over-dramatizing when he should have been under-playing, and vice versa. The fact, also, that he privately never felt absolutely certain of wanting to be leading suitor for Myra's hand was equally of no importance. For the benefit of all whom it might have concerned, the public mask which he had seen fit to adopt was that of leader and lover, and in the absence of any better – or even any other – marital prospect, Monty was damned if he'd tolerate having it wrenched from his face by any fingers other than his own.

After almost ten minutes of jerky driving he reached the outer world and began to feel free at last of Waterford and all its irksome contagions. He put his foot down, making the speedometer jump up to sixty, and, without slowing, lowered the driving window completely. He was immediately assailed by a gush of cool air that made the sun's heat doubly welcome. It shone from high over his driving shoulder, beating down in glints and flashes on the car and the roadway before him. He turned his face for a moment and threw it a look of reflected warmth. Slowly he was beginning to thaw out, get in the groove. He would put Waterford behind him – metaphorically as well as literally. Let it and Diamond Jim and his daughter stew in their own juices until he returned on Friday night. Monty wasn't going to worry about them. He wasn't going to let them spoil his week. He wasn't even going to think of them. Thoroughly self-satisfied at last, he switched on the radio and proceeded to drown its strains with his own elephantine accompaniment.

Time passed. Mile after mile whisked away beneath him as he drove, keeping the speedometer teetering around sixty. Actually, Monty had two driving speeds: a canny forty when his father was in the car, otherwise it was anything goes. The difference between the speeds was more than just an assertion of Monty's freedom of choice. It was a proven stratagem, which, since all his journeys were planned and arranged by his father on a forty m.p.h. basis, added up, week after week, to at least half a day filched from his allotted working time. In a hard-driving year that could mean anything up to an extra month's holidays. Admittedly, there were days when the bonus was of no help, for a few wintry hours saved from the early afternoon in a puddle-pocked, deserted little town were more a disadvantage than otherwise. But today, in high summer, the practice paid off. The first stop on his itinerary was the seaside town of Youghal, and as Monty licked his dry lips and adjusted the sun-block above the windscreen, he could almost inhale the ozoned breezes being wafted nearer and nearer, hear the churning waves breaking on the sands, see in his mind's eye the scads of bikinied girls, frisky, careless, devilment-primed.

Due into Youghal at approximately four o'clock, Monty reached the beginning of its seafront a few minutes before two, having skipped lunch and kept his foot down all the way over the final twenty miles. His entry into the resort was, however, as languid and decorous as that of a summer-booked spinster, being conducted at little more than walking pace, the better to scan the promenade and beach and note the talent on display. But his examination yielded next to nothing, for at such an hour almost everybody was at lunch. Monty was unperturbed – he knew that before long life would return to the deserted sands, and when it did, he would be in the thick of it. Already, without any conscious decision registering in his mind, he had put away all thought of work. With four days of the week to go, Monday could always be made expendable – which, to Monty's way of thinking, was the best thing to do with it.

He drew up at an hotel on the front and went in for lunch. In its dining-room almost all the luncheon guests had finished and departed, leaving behind tables so bedraggled and strewn with the wreckage of meals that they appeared as so many pieces of flotsam on the sea of carpet beneath. In the corner of the serving entrance was a knot of waitresses like a rescued crew who had gone through an exhausting ordeal and were waiting, wilted and squeezed, to be relieved at their posts. Monty scouted around for a clean table. There was none anywhere and so he sat at the least shambled one. The waitresses regarded him silently for quite some moments before a tall blonde girl reluctantly left the group and motored herself towards him, picking up a menu from another table on the way. She coasted to a stop by his side, giving his slightly guilty smile a freezing expression, and murmured audibly to herself, 'After the ball!'

Monty studied the menu emptily, knowing full well

beforehand that his lunch would boil down to the usual one of eggs and chips. He would not take any meat outside home, clinging rather atavistically to the Jewish dietary laws, and from experience he had learned not to gamble on the age of fish served in hotels on a Monday.

'Eggs and chips,' he said, looking up, 'and peas. And coffee – hot coffee. And I suppose I'd better order my sweet too and save you a journey.'

He took another look at the menu.

'Gooseberry pie, I think.'

'Sorry, 'soff.'

'Oh! Well then, apple tart.'

'Tha's off too.'

'Is anything on?' Monty enquired heavily.

'Rhubarb and custard. Plenty of that.'

'I'm not surprised. My favourite dish – I don't think! Never mind, bring me a dollop of it.'

The waitress shrugged and taxied back to her stand. Monty cast a practised eye over her retreating figure but it could not kindle his interest. The limpness of the too-often-washed black dress accentuated the fatigue of the girl's slouching progress and robbed her shape of its natural contours. Monty's mind darted to another female shape, that of Myra Rhinegold. Plenty of contours there – if you didn't mind double portions. He would have preferred something more slinky, but when the double portions ran to her money also – well, one would have to make some compromise. At least it was a sort of compensation for his cruelly restricted field of choice.

His meal arrived and he bent to it automatically, his mind still absent in Waterford. It had slipped away from Myra and on to her father. Rhinegold had never liked him – Monty had no illusions on that score. Nor had he any illusions as to the reason for Ape-Face's antipathy – it was pure snobbishness, nothing else. He was afraid Myra might insist on marrying Monty, and in Pot-Belly's estimation a *viklanik* wasn't good enough for Myra. With his money he could buy her a solicitor, a barrister, a doctor, a

49

biochemist, any man as long as he had a degree. But a *viklanik* – and a native of Waterford – pouf!

It was as much his ill-concealed opposition as his money that kept Monty in the chase. Myra was all right really – apart from the bit extra she dragged on to the scales – but if Monty had been in love with her he would have gone in and won long ago. As it was, he courted her only when he was in the mood or at a loose end or if there was nothing better on the horizon – or when he reassessed for the *n*th time Barrel-Bottom's wealth and imagined the explosion that would ensue if the old bloater were forced to face the prospect of some day having, in the very same breath so to speak, both to depart this life and enrich Monty Levinson almost beyond measure.

He was still mulling over the situation when he finished his lunch and emerged from the hotel into the afternoon sunlight. The sight that greeted him banished Waterford and Waterford's worries from his mind and put him right with himself. Across the road, over the prom wall, the beach and sea were visible – snarling, giant waves far enough out to be rendered innocuous as they smacked themselves down to lacing ruffles of surf that hissed back and forth like playful kittens, threatening from a safe distance the lines of stretched-out basking forms. Every moment brought new arrivals down from the guest houses hunched up the hill overlooking the front. They were so thick on the road that traffic could only crawl, honking forward in fits and starts. The sky was flame blue, unsullied anywhere, and the sun, little off dead centre, was burning its way forward.

Monty lit a cigarette and strolled over to the sea wall. He rested his elbows on it and threw his gaze far and wide over the sands, like an angler casting his bait in many directions and places to find the most rewarding spot.

Oh, but the fish were appetizing! The tide was out and so the figures bathing at the moment were too far away for close scrutiny, but on the beach below there was a wide field of choice. His eye roved from group to group, discarding the well-chaperoned and those completely alone. The former would be too closely guarded by others, the latter too closely guarding themselves. His most likely mark was just a pair of girls on their own, for Monty knew that the female sense of competition aided by the increase in daring two girls together experience when confronted by a single, defenceless male would render a pick-up all the easier. He was looking for two who were attractive, about eighteen or nineteen, already in their togs, and betraying the tell-tale desire for attention that was marked by continually thrown nervous glances at all young men either passing or lounging above them on the wall. At length Monty had made his pick – a red-headed, lithe-looking mermaid in a green, scaly costume accompanied by a raven-haired slip of a piece whose pocket size and dinky fittings inside her black bikini intrigued him. Their eyes had already locked as he scrutinized the pair and the 'Wanted' sign had flashed long enough for him to pick up the message. He sent out a testing signal in reply.

'What's the water like?' he shouted.

'Lovely,' the redhead called back. 'Why don't you come down and try it?'

'I'm on my way.'

Quickly he stubbed out his cigarette and went back to the car. On the rear seat were the cases and parcels of his various samples – sheets, cloths, napkins, towels, ties, hose, pillowcases, cushion covers, tea cosies, handkerchiefs, scarves, etc., etc., and, in a small box whose position he had carefully noted during the morning's packing, bathing trunks. Monty deftly extracted the box from the pile above it and ripped it open. He riffled through the various samples and drew out a deep purple pair. Then he tore a hole in one of the brown-paper parcels and chose a striped towel. He locked the car, pocketed the keys, and with togs and towel draped around his neck in his best Championship-hardened manner, jogged back across the road and down on to the beach.

'Smashing day,' he commented by way of conversational

opening as he lowered himself on to the burning sand next to the girls.

'Smashing,' the green mermaid agreed enthusiastically, as easily as if Monty were an old friend. 'But I wish I could get a tan. I never tan. I might turn pink. But that's all. Not like Amy – she gets black.'

Monty turned to the little raven, Amy. He saw her throw a dark, glinting look of annoyance at her friend for being so talkative and revealing her name. The look flashed out like a tiny dagger to its target, and the mermaid, by way of redeeming the position or at least plucking the blade out of her flesh, hastily said, 'My name's Alice. What's yours?'

There was a little pleasure-boat cruising past them quite near the beach. Monty read its name on the prow, *King Alfred*.

'Alfred,' he said, 'Alfred King – but all my subjects call me Your Majesty.'

Alice laughed. Amy turned on her stomach as if in renunciation of both of them. Monty wasn't sure yet how to handle her but he was in no hurry.

'Been in the water yet?' he asked.

'This morning,' Alice replied, sitting up on her knees in an excess of friendliness. 'But I'll go in again if you will.'

'Soon maybe.' Monty took out his cigarettes and offered them. Alice accepted one. Amy declined with an almost imperceptible shrug.

'Don't mind her,' Alice said in apology, risking a veritable fusillade of daggers, 'she's moody sometimes.'

Amy, the back of whose head had been turned to Monty, now turned away from Alice, and Monty was able to see her properly. Her small brown face with its slit mouth and deep eyes brooded heavily. He looked down at her.

'What's the time?' he asked.

'Why don't you look at your watch?' she replied.

'Because I know the time. I just wanted to hear you speak. I thought you'd lost your tongue.'

Monty took off his shirt and lay back beside her to let the sun play on him. There was a good deal of fat on his body and his stocky build did not quite disguise the extra weight. But he was, at least, already well-tanned and there was no break in colour between his swarthy face and brown, beefy shoulders.

'Where you from?' Alice asked. 'You're not Cork anyway – I can tell by your accent.'

'And you are,' Monty parried.

'Dublin?'

'No.'

'The North?'

'Not likely.'

'Well, where?'

'Try again,' said Monty, aware that Amy, though silent, was following the exchange. '*You* have a go,' he invited her.

'I couldn't care less,' she responded with exaggerated fatigue. 'You look foreign to me.'

'I know,' Alice jumped. 'You're Spanish! That's why you're so dark. I've seen Spanish sailors down in Kinsale. They come in there a lot.'

Monty smiled and pretended to be engagingly coy. It was not the first time he had been taken for a Spaniard. His swarthiness, his jet-black hair with its fat curls, eyes which he could heat at will to a smouldering fire, and the shadow of Semitic angularity in his features not yet rubbed completely smooth by age or fat, all helped to encourage the impersonation. It had often proved a useful bait, and to supplement it he had developed a confident and rapid line of verbal hieroglyphics that passed for the Spanish language.

'*Si, senoritas,*' he said with a little bow, '*escaludos de archipelagos semipanties decimale.*'

'Ooh,' Alice cried, overwhelmed beyond recall, 'what does that mean?'

But Amy was not convinced. Her eyes were bearded in half-doubt. Monty, sensing the delicacy of the situation, did not overplay.

'Oh, it only means "How clever of you to guess!" '

'Spanish!' Amy disparaged. 'With that name – Alfred King!'

Monty, disarmingly turning the other cheek, replied politely, 'Alfred King is the English of my name – Alfonso Armadillo Cinquecento de Kinsetta – Alfred King. Could you suggest a better alternative?'

The ploy worked. Amy sat up.

'Were you born in Spain?'

'Sure – in Toledo.' He had learned from previous experiments that Madrid, Barcelona, and Seville, already popularized by revolutions, music-hall songs, oranges, and Hollywood extravaganzas, were all too obvious choices and weakened the story. 'My father was Spanish and my mother Irish. I grew up there until the family moved over to Ireland when I was ten.'

'Where in Ireland?' Amy asked.

'Waterford.'

'How is it you haven't forgotten your Spanish?' said Alice, who had suddenly become subdued. It was as though once Amy had condescended to enter the conversation, Alice knew she had to retire to the wings.

'I still speak it with my father, of course,' Monty answered. '*Casamante a saleras e escudos frigirifico.* That means "We honour our mother tongue and the traditions of home". You know, there's always been a strong bond between the Spanish and the Irish.' He gave Amy a wink as he said this. But he had misjudged the pace.

'I know,' she retorted, 'don't tell me. You just want to make it a bit stronger, isn't that so?'

Monty immediately changed gear, pretending to be offended but to be hiding the hurt. He turned his attention back to the mermaid. In a few minutes his tactic was rewarded: Amy poked her way back into the conversation, asking, 'Are you here on holidays?'

'No. Just passing through. Are you two staying?'

'Yes,' said Amy. 'We have a room together.' She smiled for the first time, showing teeth that were like little chips of white china. Monty crowded on sail, knowing that a second rebuff so soon after the first was unlikely.

'I'll be staying the night. Not leaving till the morning. Will you be around tonight?'

'We're always at the Amusements. There's nowhere else to go except dancing and we were there last night.'

Monty accepted the information without fuss. He had completed lap one successfully. Now he leaned back and allowed the current to waft him along.

'How about a swim?' he suggested, already getting up and locking the towel around his buttocks to tog off.

The girls were enthusiastic. Tactfully they raced towards the water, Alice shrieking and laughing, Amy lagging a little behind with pattering steps. Monty took his time, watching them go down, knowing that Amy was aware of his eyes studying her. From the distance she looked no bigger than a baby. When he had his trunks on and his clothes folded he commenced to walk after them, breaking halfway into a trot that needed but one degree more of list on either side to transform it into a waddle.

They stayed in the water for about half an hour, cavorting and splashing. Afterwards, drying themselves in the heat of the sun, Monty felt he was firmly established. He spent the rest of the afternoon spinning yarns, indulging in his favourite pastime of impressing female company, expanding his personality like a gay and tuneful melodeon. His manner had the casual, practised ease of a man whose money is made and fortune secured. By the time he was ready to depart, Amy was a different person from the sullen, held-in girl who had started the afternoon by rebuffing him. She had become gay, vivid, exciting, promising. Monty knew that in her mind she was plotting how to ditch Alice for the night. He left her his most equatorial smile and a final flourish of his native tongue.

'*Hasta la vista, senoritas. El seguedillas de carburedo e candiment chiropody.*'

'What does that mean?' Amy asked.

He put his mouth to her warm ear. 'Tell you tonight,' he whispered, and departed forthwith.

Slowly he drove to his hotel in the town's business centre. Drawing up in front of its porticoed exterior, he took up his travelling bag and made for the entrance. The sun's rays, coming from three-quarter way down the sky, were able to play fully into its hall, brightening what would otherwise have been a long, gloomy corridor.

Monty approached the reception desk and whistled at the girl sitting there behind a typewriter. She looked up and immediately jumped to her feet, giving him an intimate smile.

'How'ya, Nellie!' he said as he signed in.

'Hullo, Monty. Back to the old dump! Just get in?'

'No. I've been on the beach for the past few hours. Had to have a bath before seeing you.'

Nellie laughed. Her well-shaped figure inside a yellow blouse thrust itself towards Monty as she leaned forward teasingly.

'I was on the beach too. A pity I missed you.'

'Weren't you working?'

'I just started. I'm on late shift tonight.'

'Aha,' Monty sounded meaningly. 'Very interesting.'

'I suppose you'll want a little glass of milk and biscuits before you go to sleep?'

'What do *you* think, sister?'

He gave her a leering wink as he took his room key and turned away.

'Oh, your letter, Monty,' Nellie called to him. 'I nearly forgot. This came for you just before.'

'A letter? For me?' Monty couldn't imagine who could possibly write a letter to precede him to Youghal.

'Express delivery,' said Nellie as she handed it to him.

Monty immediately recognized the grained blue envelope and the handwriting. It was Myra's.

He forgot Nellie and hurried up to his room, quickly dumping his bag and settling on the bed to open his letter.

Dear Mr Levinson, he read, and his heart went under a cold shower – such a form of address from Myra was a storm warning.

I really shouldn't lower myself by writing to you but your behaviour tonight was so disgraceful that I cannot let a week pass before telling you so. Besides, I doubt if I shall want to see you again anyway. I don't know what you think I am, but whatever it is, I'm not. Of course, you probably behave like that all the week with the common trolls you pick up in the country. But I thought that as a Jewish boy paying attention to a Jewish girl, you would know how to behave. You certainly had me fooled. You're the same as all men. You're all members of the W.H.S., which I'm sure a person of your education would know is the Wandering Hands Society. You ought to be thoroughly ashamed of yourself and I hope that if the slap I gave you did not make you realize it, this letter will. I am very disappointed that someone I have known all my life and from whom I expected better should have tried to take advantage of me as if I were a common woman of the streets.

I will close this letter now but I cannot say 'Yours sincerely' or 'Yours faithfully' because that would be hypocrisy.

Myra Rhinegold

Monty threw the letter aside and made a rude face at the wall. He knew Myra had been annoyed, but not *that* annoyed. He had had the slap coming to him – fair enough, he hadn't complained. But a letter – and this kind of a letter!

Monty took it up again and scanned it a second time. She couldn't be joking, could she, just taking a rise out of him. He extracted some of her comments and read them over, letting them ring against his ear and listening for their note. Rather sharp, even under the circumstances. 'Mr Levinson.' *Mr.* A bit thick. And that allusion to his behaviour on his travels – that was uncalled-for. And only guesswork anyway. She couldn't substantiate it. Bloody cheek, getting so personal. He should never have made a practice of telling her what towns he was visiting each week and the hotels he stayed in. Then she wouldn't have been able to send him such a letter. But he'd give her a reply that would shiver her fat *derrière* – even if it cooked his own goose altogether.

Monty ducked down to the commercial room, grabbed a few sheets of notepaper and an envelope from the rack, and sped back upstairs. Now for you, Miss Rhinegold. Miss Rhinegold, yes, that would do for openers. Or better still, Madam. *Dear Madam*. He wrote down the two words and then paused.

What if she *was* only having him on? In that case a smart letter from him might spoil both the joke and his chances. And then the whole vista was suddenly whipped away as a new idea struck him. Monty laid down his pen in wonderment. Supposing – just supposing – that Myra's letter was a trick to make him hurry up and propose to her? It was possible. She must be aware he could be considering a proposal. And he *was* the leading suitor – not to mind being also her favourite one. He'd bet on that against anyone. So maybe she thought she'd pressure him into action. A glint entered Monty's eye. If that was what she was up to, he'd soon show her who was boss. He was going to make up his own mind about his own future in his own time.

He took up his pen again and waved on the line of waiting words.

Dear Madam,
    This is hardly the time or means in which to discuss the subject of your letter. (Ah, that was a good opening. That would stiffen her excess baggage.) *I cannot, however, refrain from pointing out that some of your remarks were hardly those I would expect from the kind of lady you consider yourself to be.* (Grand, a lovely echo of her own tone.) *Furthermore, the innuendo to which you stoop in some of them is most uncalled-for and even libellous.*

58

Monty paused to consider the last two words. Were they a bit risky? He scored his pen through them and then, as they were still readable, blocked them in a square. Instead he added, *and I would not lower myself to your level by answering your charges*. (Beautiful – sparring her off at a distance with a series of rapid straight jabs. No need to come to grips at all on the subject of his behaviour with her. Now, how to polish her off?) *In any case, pressure of work prevents me from writing any more than these few lines*. That should put her in her place. Maintaining the dignified tone Monty ended with *Yours faithfully*, followed by his full name.

He read the letter over, sealed it in the envelope, wrote the address, stuck on a stamp, and put it in his pocket to post that night. Then, dismissing the subject from his mind with the air of one who has more important projects on hand, he went to unpack, looking forward to his date at the Amusements with the neat little Amy.

His unpacking did not take him very much time. Exotic blue-toned pyjamas were dumped on the bed and his toilet accessories and electric shaver put in the bathroom. Left in his overnight bag were a few shirts, two or three pairs of socks, some underwear and handkerchiefs, and, tucked under them at the bottom, his prayer-book, skull-cap, and phylacteries. The latter holy pieces were always packed as a matter of course, for he had to maintain the pretence to his father that he assiduously put on the phylacteries each morning and recited his prayers. It was a ritual he observed at home because he had to, but it was one of the first habits he had dropped when he started travelling. It had lingered for only a few weeks, having been finally discarded when a chambermaid, entering his room unbidden one morning, had found him attired in his full praying harness and had hastily fled, shrieking with horror. Monty never used the phylacteries or prayer-book again in the country – nor did he return to the same hotel. The former change cost him no regrets or twinge of conscience; the latter, however, he thought a pity, for it brought to a sudden and

59

unsatisfactory conclusion the campaign he had been conducting for the casual affections of the hotel manager's perky young daughter.

Two hours later, fed, shaved, washed, spruced, and his car checked for a sufficiency of petrol to cover the contingency of any long softening-up run that might become necessary, Monty was down at the Amusements, strolling among the holiday crowds, a keen eye alert for his date. The evening was still sun-bright and warm, shredded with the voices of the thronging merrymakers and the music of the public address, sieved with the hushing swish of the waves that, now unwooed by bathers, practised automatically against the prom wall. He had not long arrived when a hand was pressed on his shoulder and he turned to see Amy standing behind him in a flaring green skirt and buttoned white blouse, smiling – and all alone.

'Ah,' said Monty, hastily remembering his role, '*buenos noces, senorita*. Where is your friend?'

'She's not coming down. Washing her hair or something.'

'Very wise too,' Monty commented. 'Cleanliness is next to godliness.'

'What would you know about godliness?' Amy quipped.

'That depends purely on the time of day.'

Monty felt good. It was obvious that Alice had been deliberately left behind, and if he was any judge, the correct note of anticipatory tension had been sounded.

'Do you want to stay here or go out for a drive?' he asked. Routine opening attack.

'We'll stay here for a while and drive later.' Routine opening defence.

Monty did not rush things; the night was young. A bag of sweets for the lady, an ice cream, a compliment, a comradely arm to guide her through the knots of people, a promissory squeeze of the waist or hand to provide the overtones at selected moments. Within an hour they had visited every stall and left it his mead of coins. They had thrown rings, shied balls, rolled pennies, compared

60

fortunes, filled slots, shot guns, and whooped their lungs out on the chairoplanes. Their gaiety had increased as the sun declined. It was time to move on. They sensed it together and made for the exit.

'Oh, just a few tickets before we go. We may be lucky.' Amy had stopped at the brightly lit, prize-heaped stall where numbers were sold.

'Sure,' Monty said, buying her a handful as a valedictory gesture to the spirit of the carnival.

They waited among the pressing ranks of customers until the touts had sold all their tickets. The light on the board went up, the huge arrow whirled around, its propellers whirring like a butterfly's wings. The crowds were silent as the yellow flicker raced up and down the numbers. Little starts and cries volleyed forth as the arrow's progress got slower and slower, stretching people's hopes to breaking point. Then shrieks of disappointment as number after number was snuffed out, each more agonizingly slowly than the one preceding it. Finally one number, thirty-two, stayed aglow.

Amy jumped. 'We have it,' she shouted, waving her tickets. Monty eagerly confirmed it for himself. That was a stroke of luck!

'Well, take whatever you want,' he said.

'Oh, I couldn't. You bought the tickets.'

'Don't be stupid. It was your idea and I bought them for you. Go on – take your pick.'

'Well, if you insist. Anything?'

'Of course. Anything at all.'

The major-domo was before them, anxious to help.

'Yes, miss. What'll it be? A set of dishes, a beach ball, a carving knife, a teddy bear, or a pound note? You can have a pound note into your palm if you like.'

Amy hesitantly raised her hand and pointed. 'I think I'd like that statue.'

The major-domo's face lit up and the people near them made commendatory remarks. Monty went white with shock.

'Our Lady you mean, miss? The statue of the Virgin, is it?'

'That's right,' said Amy.

The major-domo leaned over and carefully took the blue-robed, gilded statue, respectfully matching its pious, sanctified, downcast expression. He proffered it to Monty.

'Here y'are, miss. The gentleman will carry it for you.'

Monty gave a start of dismay, then reddened and checked himself. Mortified, he allowed the statue to be placed into his cradling arms. He was speechless with confusion.

Amy's eyes were glowing with delight at her acquisition. They hurried to the car, Monty welcoming the opportunity to recover his aplomb. It was unlikely that any acquaintance or customer would have seen him and once the ordeal was over he found himself appreciating its humour. He realized, however, that it would not be clever to treat the situation with other than the same humility and cotton-wool respect Amy had shown. He only hoped it had not altered her mood and that the Virgin Mary would have the grace not to play gooseberry. As a precaution, he placed it on the back seat, making room for it among the samples there and padding its behind with a parcel of nylons.

'Just to make sure it won't get broken,' he told Amy.

'Yes,' she said. 'I'd have no luck if anything happened to it.'

Neither would I, Monty thought to himself as it lay quietly in a corner, its suffering eyes encompassing them.

'I think', said Amy after a moment's consideration, 'you should turn its face around. It doesn't feel right to have it looking at us.'

Monty obeyed with alacrity. He was only too glad to satisfy the susceptibilities of both his passengers.

He turned back to the wheel and slowly drove away, feeling set again and in control.

'We won't go far,' he said.

'No, not too far,' she replied.

'I meant in distance,' he added hastily.

'Did you?'

It was after ten o'clock, lighting-up time all across the sky;

Monty was aglow with anticipatory confidence. Within minutes they'd be out of the town and there were plenty of dark roads and leafy lanes around Youghal, no shortage of secluded spots in which to park.

'This is where our digs are,' Amy suddenly said as he turned into the road behind the seafront houses. 'Just up here on the left. Number twenty-seven.'

'I suppose Alice is tucked up in bed by now.'

'I suppose so. I feel a bit mean leaving her on her own. Perhaps I should just drop in and tell her I won't be late,' Amy suggested.

'But if she's in bed you might only wake her up,' Monty said, preferring not to have his programme interrupted.

'Oh no, she always reads in bed – for hours. Besides,' Amy added, turning to check on the Virgin Mary, 'I'd prefer to take the statue in. Just in case, you know. It could easily get broken there.'

'OK,' Monty responded as he pulled up outside Amy's digs. He wasn't worried about the statue getting broken but he'd be just as pleased not to have it poking into him if he managed to entice Amy into the back seat. Perhaps that was what she had in mind herself.

'I won't be a tick,' she promised as he lifted the statue out to her. He smiled and she scuttled up the path and in the door.

He lit a cigarette and waited. The cigarette was almost smoked and he was still waiting. He threw it out the window, trying not to face his doubts. She was certainly taking her time, but then she was probably dolling herself up. Girls somehow always managed to take ages doing that. The house was dark, not a light showed in it.

He took out another cigarette, then put it back in the packet, then glanced at his watch. It was at least five minutes since she had gone in. Nearer ten.

Monty sighed. There was no use pretending, no use hanging around any longer. He had been had. Amy wasn't coming back. She'd had all the fun she wanted out of him – and the ruddy statue to boot.

63

He thumped the steering wheel in disgust and disappointment, castigating himself with *'Ah caramba'*. *Hasta la vista*, indeed! These damned women, you never knew where you were with them. Smarting with annoyance he turned the car back towards his hotel.

'Monday,' he growled savagely as he prepared to go in, 'bloody Monday. I hate Mondays. They should be abolished.'

Drained both of energy and enthusiasm, he trudged up the steps into the hall. Nellie was still behind the reception desk, reading a paper, and he threw her a tired wave as he passed.

'Oh, Monty,' she called, 'there's been a man phoning for you all night. From Waterford. He phoned three times already.'

Monty's mouth fell and he drew in his breath with alarm.

'My God! Who? Who?'

'How should I know? He didn't leave a name.'

'What did he want?'

'He wanted you. He phoned at eight, at nine, and then just a while ago, at ten. Very sore he sounded. "Where *is* he? What time are you expecting him back?" '

'What did you say?'

Rhinegold, it must have been old Rhinegold. Monty could imagine him working himself into one of his special flaps, jumping up and down like a screeching gorilla.

'What do you think I said?' Nellie replied. 'I told him I knew nothing about you.'

'Well, if he rings again, you still know nothing. Tell him I'm not here, that I didn't come back, I checked out. Tell him I'm dead.'

'OK,' Nellie laughed as Monty rushed off to his room.

He undressed feverishly, violently disturbed. His night had been wrecked, the whole blissful mood shattered, first by Amy, now by this. What the hell could be up? Rang three times. It couldn't be his father. He always went to bed early. It *must* be Rhinegold. Myra must have told him. Monty suddenly screwed up his eyes in frustration as he remembered his reply to her, lying in his pocket, unposted. Damn! But maybe it was just as well. He could post it next day if nothing else happened and if he still felt like it. Perhaps Rhinegold would keep ringing all night.

Monty bundled up his clothes, drawing on his pyjamas hastily, as if bed could be his only refuge. Blast! What had Sour-Hog to get so excited about? His daughter was still all in one piece, wasn't she?

Monty fell on to the bed, exhausted now by his own panic and too flustered to realize that whatever it was that Rhinegold wanted him for – if indeed it *was* Rhinegold – he was safe and out of reach for the rest of the week, separated from his fate by miles and miles.

'Ohoho,' he crooned, half-convincing himself that he felt like crying.

Suddenly there was a knock on the door.

Monty went rigid, huddled on the edge of the bed. Good God! Not Rhinegold, come all the way for him?

'Who is it?' he called quaveringly.

The door opened swiftly and silently. Nellie darted in, carrying a glass of milk on a plate.

'Oh, you,' Monty sighed in relief. 'But I didn't want any milk. Didn't you know I was only joking?'

Nellie shut the door and locked it. She put the glass down.

'Of course I knew. But I had to have some camouflage. Good, you're all ready for bed.'

She rushed at Monty and bowled him over on to the blankets.

'No, Nellie, no, not tonight. I'm too tired,' he wailed.

Nellie laughed excitedly, seeking places to tickle his curled-up body, throwing herself on top of him.

'Come on, come on! I must be quick in case anyone is looking for me.'

She wrenched him around and pressed herself against him.

'Stop it, stop it! Get out! Get out, Nellie! I'm too tired. Not tonight.' Monty struggled and fought her, drowned in

65

the horror of the moment. He couldn't, just couldn't. The last thing he felt like after all the disappointment and shock was a hectic session.

Her strong arms were grabbing him as he twisted and turned, unable to throw her off.

'Quick!' he whispered suddenly to her. 'Stop, quick! I hear someone!' It was only a ruse to break her advantage, but as she paused and cocked an ear, Monty heard footsteps along the corridor. 'There, I told you,' he said.

'Jesus!' she shrieked, springing up and executing a frantic cross on her bosom. 'That might be the boss.' She smoothed her dress and darted to the door. With a single movement she had turned the key, opened the door, and was on the threshold.

'Good night, Mr Levinson,' she said with studied formality, for the benefit of anyone in the offing. Immediately she had shut the door Monty ran and locked it.

'Thanks be!' he breathed in relief, tottering back to the bed, his chest heaving with the effort of his exertions. Pitying himself, feeling in an orgy of despair, he switched off the light and got in between the sheets.

Blissfully he stretched his legs and then suddenly jumped as if stung. He leaped out, kicking something in the darkness as he did so, and flung on the light. The glass of milk that Nellie had left on the floor had been upset by his foot and was streaming all over the carpet. But Monty went at his bed, tearing off the covers to see what mouse or rat or awful intruder had gnawed at his toe. There, placed carefully at the bottom of the sheet, its prongs turned out, was a wire brush. It was the last straw. Completely defeated, punch-drunk, throwing in the towel, he folded up on to the wreckage of the bed, overcome by the night's shattered debris.

'Of all the stupid, dizzy, sex-starved bitches,' he wailed. 'Boo-hoo-hoo!' In an excess of emotion he sat there, his feet in a pool of milk, rocking like a mourner, telling himself that life was lousy, and even managing, by putting out maximum effort, to squeeze from his eyes a few thin, watery tears.

St Patrick Was a Jew?

I was nine at the time, my father about ninety-nine – or so it seemed to me. He had a bushy white beard that was like a second layer of the woollen pullover protecting his catarrhal chest, and the bottom of his equally bushy moustache was a perpetual nicotine brown. Indoors a white *yarmulkah* clung precariously to the back of his balding head; out of doors it rested snugly under his black bowler.

I spent as much time as I could with him in his small picture-framing factory under our home. I loved the smell of glue that always hung in the air and the carpet of coloured wood-shavings that were like leaves shed by the forest of tall, shiny mouldings leaning against the walls.

Inside the ramshackle office at the back he would sit at an untidy roll-top desk doing his bills and accounts while I explored the cupboards and drawers all around. The wide, shallow drawers housed hundreds of glossy prints which he framed and sold to shops and dealers all over the city and county. I found magic in them, not because they had come from far-off Switzerland – wondrous though that was – but because of their exotic subjects and rich, throbbing hues. Some of them were what my father called 'scenes' – sheep grazing serenely, swans riding their mirror-image on a placid river, the farmyard's seasons, mountains against a dramatic sky – but the ones that I returned to again and again were the 'holy pictures'. Their names added to their mysterious spell – Infant of Prague, The Agony in the Garden, Perpetual Succour, Virgin and

Child, and the most intriguing one of all, Sacred Heart. It depicted a handsome, sharp-featured man, bearded, his head, shoulders and chest filling the large canvas, his face looking down and slightly sideways with an expression that, if it wasn't actually absent-minded, appeared to betray no great concern. I wondered at his seeming indifference to his terrible injuries – not only was his brow blood-spattered from the band of thorns that encircled his head, but there was a big hole in his chest to expose a swollen, lurid heart.

I knew who he was of course, for I had seen another picture of him hanging in every classroom at school. In that one he was nailed to a cross and wore only a large handkerchief around his willy. His face was sunk on his chest, as if he was asleep, and sometimes, when the sun came through the classroom window and spotlit him clinging to the wall, if I peered at him through half-closed eyes I could imagine that he was really stretched out on a golden strand, drying out after a dip and happily sunbathing.

'That's Jesus Christ, Daddy,' I told my father. He was always telling *me* things so I was glad whenever I had a chance to show him that I knew a thing or two myself.

'Yes,' he replied, preoccupied at his desk. 'If you say so, Ben.'

'Who *was* Jesus Christ, Daddy?'

At this my father stopped writing and gazed into space. He closed one eye for a moment and allowed a ball of cigarette smoke to roll out of his mouth.

'He was someone who tried to be all things to all men. Not a completely unusual aspiration for a Jew. We had a few like that before him and we've had a few since.'

My father's replies to my questions were frequently puzzling but this one completely baffled me. I had never known him to be wrong before, yet surely what he was saying now couldn't be correct.

'But Christ was a Catholic, Daddy,' I argued, adding, shakily, 'Wasn't he?'

He lit another cigarette and blew the smoke out over my head. I sniffed it gratefully and waited for elucidation.

'An understandable confusion, Benjamin, under the circumstances. Incorrect, nevertheless. Jesus Christ was born a Jew and died a Jew. He has even been hailed as "King of the Jews".'

'But Catholics pray to him, don't they? And they believe he was the son of God.'

'So he was, my boy, so he was.'

I sighed. Here was yet another conundrum-answer, but fortunately my sigh made my father relent and amplify.

'We're all sons of God, Ben.'

'Is God a Jew then?' I asked. I had never thought of God as being anything.

My father smiled widely with anticipation and took a huge pull on his cigarette. God and His commandments were his favourite subject. They made him happy, he always said; they'd make everyone happy if only they were allowed.

'Of course God is a Jew. Do you think I'd have anything to do with a non-Jewish God?'

By now I was beginning to feel just a little bit mad with my father. When he was in his jokey mood it was almost impossible to get a straight answer out of him.

'But if Christ was born a Jew and died a Jew, when was he a Catholic?' I was determined to keep him to the point.

'Never! He was a Jewish teacher who went around preaching the Word of God, with a few little twists of his own.'

My father stubbed out his cigarette, emptying his mouth and nose simultaneously of the last puff of smoke, and fluffed out his beard. Then he continued.

'A lot of people took exception to his influence and so they killed him. Of course killing a man for his ideas gets rid of the man, but it never gets rid of his ideas. That's something the human race hasn't even yet learned. Anyway, some time after his death, *after* his death, mind you, a band of his followers adapted his teachings and made a

69

new religion out of them. They called it Christianity –
Christianity: Christ. Satisfied?'

I nodded.

Of course I wasn't satisfied, not quite. At the back of
my mind another, much larger, problem was forming. If
Christ had been a Jew, then, strictly speaking, all the
Christians who came after him were really Jews too from
way back. The fact that they may have called themselves
something else was immaterial. The revelation made me
dizzy with shock.

Slowly I closed the drawer on the picture of Christ's
suffering Jewish heart and idly opened the one next to it.
Staring up at me was another print I had seen hanging up on
the school wall – St Patrick banishing the snakes from
Ireland. A big man, perched on a rock, wearing a curiously
shaped hat and holding a long, curiously shaped stick, he
stared into the distance while hundreds of snakes slithered
down from the rock and into the sea. I wondered how he had
persuaded them to leave. The Pied Piper of Hamelin had
got rid of the rats – and of the children too – by playing a
tin whistle, but there was no suggestion that St Patrick
played any instrument. Yet he might well have, in exactly
the same way as the Hamelin man. I had a book at home
with a picture of an Indian sitting on the ground playing a
tin whistle and in front of him a snake was weaving from
side to side, captivated by his tune. Perhaps whoever wrote
my Irish history book thought that to get rid of the snakes
by playing a tin whistle wasn't quite a dignified way for St
Patrick to do it and so it wasn't mentioned. And of course
what was important was not the business with the snakes but
the fact that St Patrick had brought Christianity to Ireland.

Suddenly it struck me that if the Irish hadn't been
Christians before St Patrick arrived, then they must – like
Jesus – have been Jews. Come to that, St Patrick had
really been a Jew too, originally!

This was an even more shattering discovery than that
Jesus himself had been a Jew. I couldn't credit it without
some authoritative confirmation.

'Daddy, before Saint Patrick came to Ireland, were the Irish all Jews?'

'Most unlikely.'

'What were they?'

'I presume they were pagans. You see, before Christianity started, not everybody was Jewish. Those who weren't Jews were pagans. That is, people who did not believe in God, but who worshipped idols and different sorts of gods.'

'I know what "pagan" means,' I protested huffily.

'Ah! My sincere apologies, Ben. I didn't mean to imply that you were ill-informed.'

I closed the drawer on St Patrick. All this baffling new knowledge was prompting even wider questions.

'If there were only Jews and pagans, and if some of the Jews became Christians, why didn't the rest of them try to turn the pagans into Jews? To make up for the ones they had lost.'

'Ah!' my father exclaimed proudly as he lit a fresh cigarette, 'that's a very intelligent question, my boy, which I shall endeavour to answer. Briefly, the early Christians believed that their religion was better than Judaism, that it was the only true faith, and so they considered it their duty to persuade as many others as possible to join them.'

'You mean, to convert them? There's a box in the lunch-room at school for us to put pennies in to pay for the African Missions – they're Catholic priests who go out to Africa to convert the savages.'

'I don't think we should call them savages, Ben. Primitives, perhaps, but that's not the same as savages. However, to continue: the Jews considered themselves the children of God. Why? Well, the story is that before any of the peoples of the earth believed in God, He asked all the different tribes, one by one, to accept His Word and live by it for ever. One by one they all refused, until He asked the Jews. They agreed. That's why we are called The Chosen People, though really it should be the other way

71

round. We should be called The Choosing People, shouldn't we?'

My father hesitated and looked at me keenly, expecting me to laugh or at least show some appreciation of his wit, but I was too engrossed in his explanation to be amused.

'Anyway,' he went on, 'the Jews probably felt that since the people with no religion had already rejected God's Word when He offered it to them, there was no point in anyone else trying to convince them. Besides, we believe that everyone has the right to find his own path to God. So we don't try to convert people.'

Before I had time to consider this piece of information, I heard a voice from the factory call, 'Boss! Boss! I'm here!' It was Hallisey.

Hallisey was my father's carrier, but the truth of the matter was that most of the carrying was done by my father and by Jessy, Hallisey's horse. My father always said that Hallisey was the bane of his life, but I liked him. I think my father did, too.

He was a small man who looked like what I imagined a land-pirate would look like. He wore a filthy sack around his middle, and on his head was an equally filthy cap, but at such a rakish angle that it perfectly complemented the cheeky glint in his eyes. He was perpetually unshaven, his cheeks and chin mottled with clusters of black spots – though how much was stubble and how much plain dirt it was hard to say. Jessy, his horse, was not unlike him. There was the same untidy forelock trying to stray down between the eyes, the same scanty acquaintance with soap and water, the same emaciated appearance.

It was the emaciated appearance that caused the running argument between my father and Hallisey.

'Look at her bones, just look at them,' my father used to protest. 'For God's sake, man, don't you ever feed the poor animal?'

' 'Pon me soul, boss,' Hallisey would answer, crossing himself in the place where his heart was supposed to be, 'but that creature eats as much as I do meself!'

72

'I can well believe that, Hallisey, for you're only a bundle of skin and bones at best. But the poor horse works a good deal harder than you do. *You* don't need much more than a pint and a sandwich inside you to sit up on top of the cart, cracking your whip. But it's the horse does the pulling. I keep telling you to feed her properly.'

Such exchanges made my father unhappy. He often reminded me that the Bible said a man should attend to his animal's needs before he attended to his own, and time and again he tried to persuade Hallisey to take his responsibilities more seriously. Hallisey, however, while crossing himself devoutly and swearing to the Blessed Virgin that Jessy was fed three times a day, never mended his ways, and the horse's bones always stuck out through her skin.

When my father left his office to attend to Hallisey, I went upstairs to finish my homework, the question of Jesus and his origins completely forgotten. My father's explanation had been clear and straightforward, so I thought no more about it. Had I done so, I might have spared myself its sequel.

That sequel came the very next day, during the history lesson in school. The lesson was about the Danish invasion of Ireland and the Battle of Clontarf – nothing to do with St Patrick at all – when suddenly, and completely without premeditation, I turned to Paddy O'Donnell beside me and whispered, 'St Patrick was a Jew.'

Paddy barely took any notice of my remark. He certainly heard it, because he jerked his head fractionally and nudged me with his elbow as if to tell me he wanted to concentrate on what the teacher was saying.

I felt impelled to go on.

'You're a Jew, too,' I insisted.

I remember at that moment being struck, for the first time in my life, by the sound of the word 'Jew'. It was sharp, like a lance. There was a venomous ring about it. I thought of other religions' names I was familiar with – Catholic, Protestant. They were ordinary words, like 'table', 'chair', 'house'. I said them to myself and they disappeared immediately; they had no echo. I hadn't before been conscious of the difference between myself and Paddy. It had been part of the natural order of things, as superficial and as unimportant as the fact that he had foxy hair while mine was black, or that he wrote with his left hand and I with my right.

'You are, you're really a Jew,' I repeated, anguishedly groping for a lifeline that would draw us together, that would deny my sudden realization of our fundamental dissimilarity.

He must have concluded that I was just trying to be funny, for he gave me another, harder, dig in the ribs and hissed, 'Are you bonkers or something?'

He was right: I *was* 'bonkers' – or something – because later, in the playground, I returned to my theme. With a doggedness as blind as it was desperate, I explained to him the true story of his origins.

He stood and stared at me, open-mouthed, his blue eyes almost sightless with bewilderment. I began to believe that I had convinced him, that once he had overcome the initial shock of my revelation he would acknowledge our common ancestry. For a moment it seemed possible. And then he demolished my argument with a single blow. Literally. He suddenly lashed out with his fist, catching me right between the eyes. I didn't at first feel any pain, any physical pain, that is; my injury was of a more lasting kind. I couldn't understand why Paddy O'Donnell, the quietest boy in the class – and one of the cleverest too – should react with such anger. And we had always got on perfectly well together. What had I said that was so outrageous?

By the time I got home after school both my eyes were beginning to blacken and swell up but the pain was still as nothing compared to the sense of grievance that by now overwhelmed me. I told my mother that I had run into a door, and I hurried through my dinner to go down and confront my father.

He listened to my story and then burst into laughter.

For the second time that day I was shocked. Bad enough that Paddy O'Donnell should hit me, but that my father should find it something to laugh at was too much.

'There's nothing funny about it, Daddy,' I shouted angrily. 'Why are you laughing?'

'*You* tried to convert *him*!' he spluttered. 'Oh, Benny, Benny, that's a rich one.'

And he kept on laughing. One hand was clasped against his side while the other tried to hold me off – in my frustration I had started to pummel his thighs with my fists. It seemed as if he would never stop when someone suddenly shouted his name from the factory and one of our neighbours' little children rushed panting into the office.

'Sir, sir, Mr Hallisey's horse is dyin', it's fallen down flat in the Main Street and Mr Hallisey can't get it up, it's dyin'.'

The words were almost incomprehensible, so madly did they tumble over themselves in the lad's excitement.

'I knew it,' my father groaned, his hilarity at my discomfiture banished with a suddenness that amazed me, 'I knew it. I knew it would happen some day. That animal is so under-nourished goodness knows what disease has struck it down.'

Quickly clamping his bowler hat on his head he ran out of the factory, myself and the messenger of ill-tidings on his heels.

Immediately he turned into North Main Street there were so many spectators gathered in the road that traffic had come to a standstill and he had to push his way through to get anywhere near the patient. He found the report had not been exaggerated. The shafts of the cart had been unbuckled and Jessy was stretched out on the road with a burly youth half-kneeling on her head. Beside him sat Hallisey, reclining on an armchair he had pulled off the cart, calmly tendering advice and instructions.

'The poor beast! The poor, sufferin' animal!' he wailed, springing up the moment he saw my father. 'What misfortune is it has fallen on her, I wonder?'

'What indeed!' my father echoed. 'And by the same

75

token, what misfortune is it that told that big oaf to sit on top of her head and crush the last of the life out of her?'

'But, sure that's only for the safety of the public, boss,' Hallisey protested, turning to the crowd as if inviting gratitude for his thoughtfulness and consideration. 'You know, if the beast kind of jumped up any way sudden and lashed out with those hooves.'

The rest of the sentence trailed away as my father very slowly paced a few circles around Jessy, examining her from every angle. The murmurs of the crowd subsided, apart from one woman who kept insisting the vet should be sent for.

'Don't move,' my father ordered Hallisey after a moment. Then he turned and pushed his way back through the spectators. They parted for him as if he had been Moses parting the waters of the Red Sea.

Within a minute he returned – carrying in his arms a bulging bag of oats. Carefully he placed the bag on the road beside the prostrate animal.

'Now, get up,' he ordered the youth holding the horse's head.

The youth got up.

So did Jessy. With a jingle of harness and a bound that would have done credit to a two-year-old, she sprang to her feet and dug her nose into the bag.

A long wail, like a siren running down, escaped from the onlookers, and my father turned angrily to Hallisey.

'Did you give the animal any breakfast this morning?' he demanded.

'Breakfast, boss? Sure she has that every morning!'

'But *this* morning, Hallisey, *this* morning? Are you sure you fed her *this* morning?'

Hallisey frowned, as if to remember so far back required a tremendous effort of concentration. Then the answer hit him.

'Ah, of course, boss, that's right. I was in such a hurry to get to work that I must have forgot. Yes, that's it – I must have forgot.'

My father grunted scornfully. 'You forgot all right. But Jessy didn't – and she just decided to go on strike until someone remembered. Look at her now!'

They both stood gazing at Jessy as she continued to eat her way into the bag of oats.

'Come along, Benjamin,' my father said, taking my hand. 'We must be getting back.'

As we reached the corner of the street we turned for a last look and saw that a policeman had appeared on the scene. He seemed to be questioning Hallisey closely, with the crowd milling around to hear what was being said. I thought my father would go back to explain what had happened, but he didn't.

'Is the policeman going to arrest Hallisey?' I asked him.

'I doubt it,' he said. 'He might summons him. That would mean Hallisey would have to appear in court, before a judge. The judge would hear the case, and if Hallisey was found guilty of neglecting Jessy, the judge would probably make him pay a fine.'

'How much?'

'Not a great deal. A few pounds or so.'

'But would Hallisey have the money to pay?'

'Probably not.'

'Would they put him in gaol then?'

'No. I'd pay the fine for him. If I didn't, he'd have to borrow from someone and that would mean he'd have even less money to buy food for Jessy.'

'You see, my son' – we were back in my father's office now, and as he spoke, the smoke from his cigarette spurted from his mouth in little jets the way Jessy's breath had shot from her nostrils when she jumped up and started to eat her oats – 'it's just a matter of doing as much good as you can. That's really all God wants of us. To be good. A long time ago, in the time of the Bible, there was a famous Jewish sage – a wise man – who was asked to sum up the Jewish faith while he stood on one foot. That meant he had to be quick about it and hadn't any time for long explanations – unlike your father. His answer was: "Do

77

not unto others as you would not have others do unto you. That is the law. The rest is commentary.'' Do you understand that?'

'Of course,' I answered. 'It's easy.'

'Ah yes, easy to understand but not always easy to remember. And forgetting it can often land you in trouble – or get you a couple of black eyes! You wouldn't have liked it if Master Patrick O'Donnell had told you *you* weren't a Jew, would you?'

'No, I wouldn't.'

'Of course you wouldn't. A man is judged by what he does, my boy, and what he does depends on what he believes.'

'So Saint Patrick wasn't really a Jew?'

My father shook his head.

I could see it now. I could see why Paddy had hit me. He was as proud of being a Catholic as I was of being a Jew.

'I'd never change my religion,' I said. 'You wouldn't either, would you, Daddy?'

My father put his head on one side and ran a hand through his beard as if he was giving the question serious consideration.

'I might,' he answered, 'I might.'

I looked at him in horror and consternation. It couldn't be! Surely it couldn't be!

'But what would you change to?' My voice was almost a whisper.

'A better Jew, my son. A better Jew,' and his booming laughter filled the office as my world fell into place again.

A Jolson Story

When Mr Levin opened his evening paper and suddenly came on the paragraph reporting the death of Al Jolson, the shock made him lower his cup of tea so forcefully into its saucer that everyone looked at him in alarm.

'*Vos iz de meisa?*' asked his father, the white strands of his beard brushing the table-top.

'Jolson is dead,' announced Mr Levin in a voice stark with horror and disbelief.

His father, whose mind after eighty years' use was daily shedding more and more needless detail, could not immediately place the name. Thinking he had heard incorrectly, he pecked about for help. '*Ver? Ver?*' looking in turn to his daughter-in-law and grandson.

'Jolson,' Leah answered impatiently. 'Al Jolson, the singer.'

'Jolson?' he repeated, still at sea, the cracking red skin of his face shrinking and creasing as he grimaced with annoyance. Then suddenly, 'Ah, Jolson, *de zinger*.' His dry blue lips opened in satisfaction and a self-congratulatory light flicked across his eyes. Jolson – that was the *shiksa*-lover with the hoarse, rough voice and *meshuggeneh* songs that came out of the records his son played. That was music? Noise. Music was the pure, winged notes that carried the Sabbath and High Festival prayers up to the Lord, blessed be His name.

He handed his daughter-in-law the tall glass from beside his plate and watched her fill it with strong black tea. Eagerly he took the glass back and dropped in a spoonful

79

of sugar and slice of lemon. And as his old eyes gazed at the crystal specks sinking down through the dark, shimmering liquid and the ring of lemon floating on top, the sight reminded him, as always, of the heavy skies and tightly closed drapery of cloud that made the sun weak and pale like a lemon-coloured moon, and of the flakes of snow that seemed to be constantly falling, falling, when he had been a young man in his parents' home in Russia.

He sipped the tea as his son read out the report of Jolson's death. Not that he was listening – he had already forgotten again who Al Jolson was – and neither Leah nor Larry was interested. To Leah, Jolson was just another singer; to Larry, he wasn't even a good one. But he had one particular distinction – he was Jewish; and that alone was sufficient to get every record he ever made into his father's collection. There was no denying Yussa Levin loved music – but he never loved it more than when it was performed by a Jewish artist. Singers, pianists, violinists, conductors, crooners, band-leaders – they were all there: the -steins and -itzskys and -ovichs, and the ones who had changed their names and whose antecedents Mr Levin avidly hunted down. That the Levins were the only Jewish family left in the town seemed not to disturb Larry's father. He had his own Jewish congregation, more numerous, more imperishable, than the one he had spent all his life with in their little Irish refuge until soul by soul it had gradually departed to bigger cities, further fields.

Larry, neither clever enough for the professions, nor sharp enough for the world of commerce, had taken his place in his father's tailoring business, shackled to the cutting-table and the hot, steaming presses. His unrelieved, companionless daily routine, his nights spent mostly in Malachy's Bar in the company of ex-schoolmates with whose idiom he was familiar but to whose world he was alien, increased his feeling of rootlessness. Jolson and Jolson's kind may have been sufficient to fill Yussa Levin's world, but Jolson alive or dead meant nothing to Larry and it was more than he could do to muster any sympathy for the singer's death. It wasn't as if his father and Jolson had been old friends or that he had ever met the man. And he still had his records – he'd always have those bloody records, so what was the great fuss about?

Larry stubbornly picked at the remains of his food until Mr Levin, conscious of his son's hostility but finding it impossible to keep his grief to himself, began to hum one of his favourite Jolson numbers. 'A great loss, a great loss,' he uttered dejectedly, in despair almost as much at the total lack of sympathy from his own family as at the death of one of his idols.

'What's the great loss?' Larry felt stung into grumbling. 'People die every day.'

His father bent forward, his eyes lighting with enthusiasm. 'But Jolson was such a singer.'

'So? Singers die every day too, and there are still plenty left.'

Mr Levin leaned back in his chair, shaking his head and spreading his hands expressively.

'No one like Al Jolson! A voice like his comes once in a lifetime. No! Once in a century!'

'A voice like his!' Larry exclaimed. 'He had no voice. He croaked!'

'Ach, what do you know about it?' Mr Levin said angrily. 'It was the way he sang, the way he put it over. "The greatest entertainer of them all," he was called. By thousands. By millions. You know better than all these people? You're a judge?'

Father and son eyed each other. Larry knew that his father was holding something back, something he wanted to say that meant more to him than anything else. And Mr Levin knew that his son was waiting for him to say it, waiting for him to trot out his old chestnut so that he could dismiss it with ignorant jeers. Let him, he thought, let him sneer, but it's true no matter what he says.

Mr Levin thrust himself forward again. 'He was a great artist,' he insisted. 'And why?' He paused as Larry's cold

81

stare held him, the corner of ridicule already showing in his eyes. But he was caught up now and had to continue. 'Yes. Because he was a Jew. Because he sang with a *Yiddishe* heart.' He sank back, his eyelids drooping with relief, his whole body relaxed as if freed of a huge burden.

Larry looked at the ceiling. 'Here we go again,' he sang out derisively.

'It's true, it's true,' his father repeated.

'But what about all the other singers, the ones who aren't Jews? Some of them are quite good too, you know. And *they* have no *Yiddishe* heart. What do you say to that?'

'I'm only talking about Jewish artists, Jewish musicians,' Mr Levin answered doggedly. 'They wouldn't be where they are today if they hadn't been Jews.'

Larry, exasperated, thumped the table. 'That's sheer nonsense. That's just a lot of racial claptrap.'

'No, it is not nonsense,' Yussa Levin shouted, refusing to give ground though he knew his argument would sharpen even further his son's scorn. 'Being a Jew means something, something special, the same as being French means something special, or being Italian, or Irish. Every race has its own gifts, its own talents. The Italians are great painters, great operatic singers too; the Germans, composers; the Russians, chess and ballet; the French, food, fashion.'

'And the Jews?'

'Take the Jews?' Mr Levin asked himself. He paused. 'Take the Jews,' he announced. Then, 'The Jews have a touch of magic, a talent for accepting the worst and making the best of it. How? I'll tell you how. They pour their sorrow into music. Music is the most powerful, the most moving expression of all. The written word is silent; art is silent; dance is silent. But music is the sound of what is in your heart. Put the Jewish heart into music and you have magic. You have a Heifetz, a Rubinstein – and an Al Jolson.'

Larry burst out laughing. 'If you ask me, all you have

there is a load of racial conceit, the kind of thinking and talking that makes people anti-Jewish.'

Mr Levin reddened. 'Is it only the Jews who love Al Jolson? Is it only the Jews who buy his records? You say I like him only because he's a Jew, but *you* seem to *dis*like him for the very same reason. What's wrong with being a Jew? Is it such a burden for you? Are you sorry already?'

Overcome with emotion, Mr Levin threw his napkin down on the table and rushed out of the room.

Larry did not move, too confused to think of what he could have said even if his father had waited for a reply. He looked at his grandfather. The ageing eyes were closed and the old man's head was nodding imperceptibly on his chest in silent recital of the Grace after Meals. Larry looked at his mother. She was scanning the newspaper his father had discarded; he knew she was long tired of an argument that always left both her husband and her son raw and unhappy. There was no answer there, no help from either of them. They had no such problems, no such questions.

Suddenly he heard the sound of music from the next room and the lush, throaty rasp of Jolson's voice cut through the wall as if to accuse him. That was his father's answer but it was more than Larry could bear. Pushing his chair back from the table, he ran out of the room and out of the house.

'You're early tonight,' Bill said. He was checking bottles behind the bar and turned round in surprise when Larry entered. 'The boys aren't here yet.'

Larry could see that. He hadn't expected to find his friends there so soon but it hadn't occurred to him that the place would be completely empty and he'd be exposed to Bill's conversation. He wasn't in the mood for chit-chat with Bill. He wasn't in the mood for talk of any sort, but where else was there to go except Malachy's and what else was there to do except drown his frustration in drink? Bill was already pouring a pint.

'Thanks,' Larry said, putting a pound note on the counter.

'You know the old saying,' Bill launched forth eagerly – he'd have little opportunity for conversation when the premises filled up – ' "the last shall be first and the first shall be last".'

Larry didn't know any such old saying; it sounded like something Bill had made up just to get the talk started. He looked at the barman beadily.

'You know,' Bill grinned, 'you're usually last but tonight you're first.' Then, seeing that his logic was lost on Larry he added, 'I expect the boys will be in soon.'

'The boys' were Tim Holland, Con O'Neill and Eddie Hegarty, three ex-schoolmates of Larry's, drawn together not so much by the mutual attraction of shared school memories as by some inhibition each one nursed that restrained him from cultivating fresh acquaintances. So they had become a mutual protection society that two or three nights a week, as the fancy took them, repaired to one of their homes for a few hours' whist, while on the other nights they grew red-faced and irascible in Malachy's until Bill's repeated calls of 'Time' sent them on their way.

Larry took his pint to a corner table, hoping his friends might agree to a whist session rather than having to drag through the rest of the night downing pints. Argument with his father always made him morose, and he knew he wouldn't be able to keep his touchiness in check throughout a long drinking session. Sooner or later he'd be bound to come to verbal blows with Tim Holland, the intellectual of the group, who liked to monopolize the conversation. Larry often suspected that some of Tim's wilder theories were intentionally provocative. O'Neill and Hegarty never had the mettle to oppose him, but Larry, though conscious that he really wasn't a match for his adversary, disliked him enough to chance taking him on now and again. When that happened, horns were locked.

This time Tim almost tempted him into opening hostilities immediately he entered the pub with Con and Eddie in tow. Affecting exaggerated surprise on seeing Larry there and already half-way through a pint, he commented loudly to Bill, 'Yer man must have been thrown out at home, is that it?'

'I dunno,' Bill responded, 'but he was the first client of the night. Wandered in here almost twenty minutes ago.'

Tim carried his pint over to Larry's table and dropped heavily in beside him.

'Wandered in, eh boy?' he joked, then turning to O'Neill and Hegarty he declaimed, 'Meet Larry Levin, boys, the original Wandering Jew!'

'There's a plant called the Wandering Jew,' O'Neill offered irrelevantly, fingering the beard he was trying to grow to give himself a more imposing look. 'Why is it called that, I wonder?'

'For that matter, why is the Wandering Jew called the Wandering Jew?' Hegarty asked. 'Why, Larry?'

'I don't know,' Larry answered impatiently. He'd had enough of the subject of Jews for one night. Then, half-ashamed to display ignorance of his own people, he said, 'I suppose it's because when the Israelites escaped from Egypt, they wandered in the wilderness for forty years.'

'Indeed and 'tis not,' Tim Holland contradicted, pushing his spectacles up in a schoolmasterish gesture that always irritated Larry. 'It's because a Jewish cobbler refused to let Jesus rest in his house when he was carrying the Cross. So the Jews were condemned to wander the earth for the rest of time.'

There the bastard goes again, Larry thought, trying to make a fool of me. He decided to ignore the story.

'Well, they made a fine job of their wandering,' O'Neill remarked. 'You'll find them everywhere. Even here.' He laughed as if he had made a joke.

'Lord above,' Hegarty exclaimed, 'who'd ever want to come to this God-forsaken place? Not even a wandering Jew.'

'They don't wander,' Larry grunted, and then with more of a rasp, 'Jews don't wander, they're driven.'

'Aye,' Holland commented, 'usually in big cars.' He took a huge swallow of his pint as O'Neill and Hegarty guffawed loudly.

Larry kept his temper. He rose from the table and went to the bar to buy a round. The pub had begun to fill up by now and while waiting to catch Bill's eye he tried to avoid asking himself what he was doing in Malachy's Lounge Bar drinking with a supercilious lout like Tim Holland and the other two numskulls. What possible affinity did he have with them? Was he going to spend the rest of his life in their company? The vision of himself buying round after round, night after night, for hundreds, thousands of nights to come could not be banished. It sent a shiver through him.

When he returned to the table they were still on the subject of the Jews.

'Tim says that Joyce said that Ireland never let the Jews in,' O'Neill informed him. 'How did you get here so, Larry? Incognito?'

'Correction, you thick!' Holland insisted. 'I never said Joyce said that. What I did say was that a character in Joyce's *Ulysses* said it. Erroneously, of course. Obviously,' and he raised his glass to Larry. Then he added, 'You've read *Ulysses*, no doubt.'

'No, I haven't,' Larry told him vehemently. He wasn't a reader, and he knew Holland knew it. It was Holland getting at him again, the way he always did, either subtly or in pretended friendly ribbing. If Larry were to challenge him Holland would be sure to say that he was imagining things, that Jews tended to have a persecution complex. And then he would probably follow that with a theory that people who suffered from a persecution complex were really suffering from an inferiority complex.

'*Ulysses*?' Hegarty speculated. 'Isn't that the book with a Jewman in it?'

'Bloom. Leopold Bloom,' from Holland. 'June 16th,

86

is Bloomsday. Your birthday isn't June 16th, is it, Larry?'

'For Christ's sake,' Larry exploded, 'can't you think of anything else to talk about but Jews?'

'No need for rancour,' Holland said. 'Is there, boys?' he appealed to O'Neill and Hegarty.

'Right there, Tim, right,' O'Neill responded predictably, always eager to take his cue. 'No need to take our Lord's name in vain.'

Larry made a derisive snort.

'What's that supposed to mean?' O'Neill asked suspiciously, a touch of aggression in his voice.

'I think what Larry means to say', Holland enunciated in his most superior tone, 'is that *our* Lord – yours and mine and Eddie's here, that is – isn't Larry's Lord and so his use, or abuse, of the sacred name casts no shadow of a blight on his soul. For him to take *his* Lord's name in vain he would have to utter the name Yahweh in a similarly derogatory fashion.'

Holland leaned back smugly, downed what was left of his pint and smacked his lips. O'Neill and Hegarty followed suit, finishing their glasses and taking up the pints Larry had bought for them. They settled back in their chairs in comfortable anticipation. Holland, too, took his second pint, held it up towards his adversary as the priest offers the Host, and gulped down half of it.

'Eh, Larry?' he invited.

Larry struggled to suppress his rising temper. Holland wasn't just taking a friendly rise out of him – he wasn't even being his usual supercilious, big-headed self. He was deliberately needling – deliberately spotlighting the divide between them. And if Larry tried to take issue with him, Holland would only out-talk him. Besides, to argue the point would only force him into making claims for himself, and that was something he kept putting off, like making a decision about what he would do with the rest of his life. He couldn't define himself, he didn't want to try to define himself – and it burst him that he had neither the will nor the ability to do so.

His absence of response sent Holland in pursuit.

'You know that part in *Ulysses*,' he said, as if Larry couldn't really be ignorant of the novel and his denial of having read it must have been just cod-acting, 'that part where Bloom is asked what his nation is and he answers that he was born in Ireland – that was fair enough, wasn't it?'

'Fair enough, 'twas,' Eddie Hegarty solemnly agreed, while O'Neill nodded sagaciously.

'Now if only you had been born in Dublin, Larry, on June 16th,' Holland continued.

Larry's lips tightened. How much more rope would Holland try to take? As much as he was allowed, for sure. Even if Larry said nothing, the other two, he knew, would not be denied their sport.

'Why so?' O'Neill asked.

'Sure your man Bloom was no more than a commercial traveller but Larry here is a tailor. That's a skilled job, being a tailor. Anyway, old Leopold is only a man in a book, while you're real flesh and blood, Larry. But sure, who knows, you might still turn out to be a more famous Irish Jew than Leopold Bloom, eh?'

But Larry didn't wait for the sycophants to bray. The insult, disguised though it was, hit his raw nerve. He jerked to his feet, shaking the table and upsetting an empty glass. He could feel the blush in his face, the heat in his blood, the tangle of emotions that made him forget all his resolve not to crack.

'I don't give a fuck for you, Holland,' he shouted. People at the bar and at other tables turned round to look. 'I don't give a fuck for Leopold Bloom, or James Joyce, or your Lord. I don't give a fuck for any of you.'

His heart pumping savagely, he barged through the thunderstruck drinkers, out the door of Malachy's, down the narrow street and around the corner before he allowed himself to rest against a wall, try to calm his heaving lungs and wipe the tears from his eyes.

He felt sick. He had had only two pints, so he couldn't be drunk, yet he felt sick. As he walked on, his only thought to get as far away as possible from Malachy's and Tim Holland, his stomach churned and each step seemed to drag a weight up like a stone from his chest to block his throat when he tried to breathe. His mind, too, was clamped in some rigid vice that froze all rational thought. He didn't know who he was or what he was. As he looked around him, for a moment he didn't even know where he was. Had he lost all physical bearings along with any sense of identity? This wasn't the way home. Then he recognized his surroundings. Somehow he had wandered off course and arrived at the little back street that housed his father's tailoring premises.

He approached the darkened window and stood before it, staring in at the dummies that posed there, immobile, their painted eyes focused back on him. They were well-groomed, as he was. They looked respectable, law-abiding, just like him. They wore good suits, as he did. All made by his father, as his was. They would stand in the window, day in, day out, fulfilling their role, as long as his father was alive.

Above the window the fascia-board bore the fading title – Y. Levin & Son, Bespoke Tailor. Larry raised his eyes to study it. 'Y. Levin.' Yes, that summed up his father – that was his father's mark. 'Y' for Yussa, the Hebrew for Joseph. His father couldn't put J. Levin on the sign, it had to be Y. Levin. There wouldn't be another man in Ireland whose first name began with 'Y' – or if there were, it would probably be another Jew. 'Y. Levin & Son.' & Son. 'That's you, boy,' Larry muttered to himself. He wished he had a ladder and a pot of whitewash to paint out that '& Son'. Not that that would solve anything.

Disgustedly he turned away and continued home. There was nowhere else to go. Certainly not back to Malachy's Bar.

As he reached the house and opened the garden gate,

already he could hear the music from the front room. Jolson again. 'Oh no,' he groaned. His father would probably spend the whole evening wallowing in an orgy of Al Jolson songs.

Inside the front door the strains of 'Sonny Boy' became clear. He grimaced. He could imagine his father's feelings listening to the words –

> *You're sent from Heaven*
> *And I know your worth*
> *You made a Heaven*
> *For me right here on earth.*

The irony of the lyric ground through Larry with its sharp edge of remorse. He could see his father, sunk into his easy chair, his head moving slowly to Jolson's rhythm, maybe even wiping tears of unhappiness from his eyes. What foolishness! Didn't his father realize that the Sonny Boy addressed in the song was a child of three? When Larry had been three . . . oh, what was the use of thinking like that? His father knew nothing of Larry's world. His father was Y. Levin – Yussa – who had spent his childhood, his youth, and most of his manhood among a Jewish community that was large enough to fill the synagogue. Now the synagogue was empty and the congregation was only to be found in the burial ground – and in the family of Y. Levin & Son. All right for Y. Levin – he was still Yussa, still part of that ghetto congregation that had begun to die before it could hold its grip on Larry Levin, son of Yussa, or he on it.

The record ended and Larry waited at the bottom of the stairs, waited to see if that was to be the end of the recital. He couldn't imagine that it would have left his father in any mood for his other Jolson favourites. 'California, Here I Come', 'Toot-Toot-Tootsie, Goodbye', 'April Showers' – they were hardly suitable to follow 'Sonny Boy', not on the day of Al Jolson's death.

Then out of the silence, the sound of yet another record *did* rise and Larry sank down on to the bottom of the stairs as he recognized the melody and remembered its spell. It was the recording by Jolson, a Cantor's son, of *Kol Nidrei*, the prayer which ushers in the most hallowed day in the whole Jewish calendar – the Day of Atonement. Hearing it reminded Larry how every year without fail Y. Levin & Son, Bespoke Tailor, was closed and the whole family travelled to Dublin to observe the Fast, how Y. Levin and his son spent the long day until sundown in the synagogue, praying and making penance, how until his own *Bar Mitzvah* at the age of thirteen he had looked forward to being allowed to enter the sacred state of being a Jewish adult and fast himself for the whole twenty-six hours, and how now the complete ritual – journey, fast, prayer, atonement – seemed to have nothing whatever to do with him. As the words of the prayer floated out, imparted by Jolson with the characteristic, time-honoured flourishes of the Jewish cantor, Larry recalled its meaning and symbolism: that all terrestrial ties of whatever sort which had been entered into for the future year were to be completely absolved and could have no force after the Day of Atonement unless renewed.

Turning to go up to his bedroom, he placed his hand on the banister, and as he looked at it he remembered another Jewish prayer: '*If I forget thee, O Jerusalem, let my right hand forget its cunning.*' He laughed. Terrestrial bonds, how are ye? Where was Jerusalem? Not in Ireland anyway, that was for sure. Bloom's words swam back into his mind. 'I was born in Ireland,' Bloom had said, 'I am an Irishman.' 'Are you now?' Larry asked. 'Are you indeed?'

He entered his bedroom and as he sat on the bed an answer – an answer of sorts – came to him. 'Go home, Leopold Bloom, all is forgiven.' It was meaningless. Just words, words. Jerusalem, Irishman, Bloom, Jew, home. There was a song, wasn't there? 'Show me the way to go home.' Did Al Jolson ever record that? he wondered.

Grand-Uncle Sopsa's Stories

Grand-Uncle Sopsa was the only one of his kind, a Jewish *shanachie*. He learned about the *shanachie* in his youth, when he used to accompany his father – my great-grandfather – on his weekly peddling trudges through the Irish country villages, and the image of the ancient Irish storyteller holding his audience in thrall around the winter fireside caught his fancy. The role suited him down to the ground, for he was a compulsive talker who never seemed to exhaust his fertile imagination. He fantasized embarrassingly in company, convincing everyone that he believed his own stories, as a result of which he gained the reputation of being harmlessly mad. Winter and summer he dressed in a sober pinstripe suit, boots polished to a sparkle, natty spats, and a grey Homburg hat. The hat never left his head, in keeping with the rule that an orthodox Jew should never leave his head uncovered, but while the other men of the community wore the traditional *yarmulkah* indoors, Grand-Uncle Sopsa wore his hat. Once, accidentally, he happened to knock it off when he was bending down to tie his bootlaces. He was quite bald, and in that moment he looked a total stranger.

The secret ridicule of the grown-ups greatly frustrated him. They were never willing listeners, and he had no wife or family whose attention he could command. That left him either to talk to himself – which he did – or to host intimate circles of nine- to twelve-year-olds made up of myself, my brothers and sisters and our friends and playmates. We were, in fact, his ideal audience – too old for fairytale, too young for disputation – and he tailored his stories accordingly. We treated them as mere entertainment, little guessing that they were more than just stories, that what he was doing was signposting the way into the real world we would all very soon have to enter. He was, I suppose, a very early exponent of the ultramodern technique of subliminal suggestion, which is probably why I can still remember many of his tales. One of them he called 'The Case of the Persecuted Cow'.

'My friends' – that was always how he commenced, not 'Children' or even 'Boys and girls' and certainly never 'Once upon a time' – 'My friends, what's the first thing your mother does when she gets up and goes downstairs in the morning, eh?'

Nobody answered. Our role was to listen, and we were used to Grand-Uncle Sopsa's habit of enlivening his narration with questions he would answer himself. Our *cheder* teacher used the very same method during the Biblical-history hour when recounting the adventures of the Israelites.

'The first thing she does', he continued, 'is to go to the front door, open it, and take in the bottles of milk from the doorstep. No?'

Yes – in silent nods.

Encouraged, he went on. 'When I was a young boy, there was no such thing as *bottles* of milk. The milkman was the farmer who owned the cows that gave the milk, and every morning he or his son would trot up to your house in his horse and cart, and if you happened to get up early enough or if your bedroom happened to be in the front of the house, you could look out the window and you'd see him there, the reins in his hand, standing up among three or four tall, gleaming churns, like a Roman charioteer surrounded by gladiators.

'He'd march up to the door, give his special knock, and your mother would be ready for him with her jug. The milkman would have a can – a very large can – in one hand, and in the other a much smaller one, just big enough to hold a pint. Then pint by pint he'd pour from the big can into the small one whatever amount your mother wanted, and from that into her jug. And before he left he'd always give her an extra drop straight from his big can. He called that "the tilly".'

We nodded knowingly to each other because the cleverest of us would have remembered from our Irish class at school that 'tilly' was from 'tuille', the Irish for 'extra'.

'Then your mother would take a cloth from her apron pocket, clean up the drops of milk that had fallen on the doorstep, and away the milkman and his horse and cart would trot – until the next day.'

Grand-Uncle Sopsa paused. His pauses always indicated that something special was coming.

'But what if next day was *Pesach*, the Festival of Passover, when all the crockery in the house and all the cutlery has to be changed, and all food has to be strictly *kosher* and the milk couldn't be taken from the same churns and cans the milkman carried every day and gave to all his Christian customers? Nowadays the milk for Passover comes from the creamery where everything is supervised by the Rabbi and the bottles left on your doorsteps have been specially scoured and filled in the Rabbi's presence and the tops of them have his special seal with *Kosher le Pesach* printed on them.'

We nodded. That was all familiar to us, taken for granted.

'But not so when I was young. When I was young somebody from each family would have to make two or three trips every Passover with his own cans, out to the milkman's farm, and watch the cows being milked straight into the cans. That way he'd be certain his family's milk was *Kosher le Pesach*. I made those trips many times.'

How exciting, we thought, wishing already that things had never changed.

'But one year – I was only seventeen at the time – a week before Passover, the farmer who was our milkman died and we had to find a new one in a hurry, and then my

mother fell ill and I had to get up early in the morning to be
ready for the new milkman and she wasn't better in time to
explain to him about our Passover milk. My father was
away in the country all that week so I had to make the
arrangements myself. Well, you might think, what of it? I
was big enough and old enough. Where was the problem?'

Grand-Uncle Sopsa took a big breath, treated us to
another of his dramatic pauses, and blew his nose before
continuing.

'The problem was that we were our new milkman's first
Jewish customers so he knew nothing about our religious
requirements and we had no idea whether he'd be willing
to agree to our strange Passover request.

'So, two days before *Pesach* I asked him.

' "Mr Corcoran," I said – I remember that was his
name, Corcoran – "Mr Corcoran, have you heard of
Passover?"

'He stopped filling my jug and looked up at the sky.

' "Did I hear what pass over, Mr Marcus?" he asked.'

We all laughed heartily, then quickly fell silent again,
anxious to hear the rest of the story.

' "No, no, Mr Corcoran," I said. "Nothing passed
over. I asked if you ever heard of Passover – the Jews'
Easter."

' "Oh, the Jews' Easter," he said. His voice sounded
confident but, my friends, never trust a man's voice. If
you want to find out whether a man is speaking the truth,
look into his eyes. I looked into Mr Corcoran's eyes
and – *ai, gevald* – I could see that he had no idea what
I was talking about. So I had to explain to him what
Pesach was and why I wished to go out myself to his farm
and supervise the milking personally during the Festival.

'He stared at me for a while and then he said, "You
mean, Mr Marcus, that you want to milk the cow
yourself?" '

Great hilarity from us, but Grand-Uncle Sopsa quickly
raised a hand for silence.

' "No, of course not," I said. "I'll just bring my cans

along and watch you milk the cow straight into them. Would you mind if I did that?''

' "And why should I mind, Mr Marcus?" '

Grand-Uncle Sopsa had drawn himself up, raising his eyebrows in surprise, his voice set to the music of a rich Irish brogue that almost convinced us we were seeing and hearing Mr Corcoran himself. Then he bent his head conspiratorially, beckoning us with a forefinger to lean forward.

'I imagine that Mr Corcoran was quite pleased to have me come and fetch the milk myself. He probably felt that if only all his customers would do the same, he wouldn't have to get up so early and he'd be saved a lot of work and travel. Don't you think so?'

We responded with a low murmur of assent and Grand-Uncle Sopsa smiled, pleased with our rapt attention. Then he resumed his role of storyteller.

' "No, Mr Marcus," Mr Corcoran said, "I don't mind at all. I'll put Eileen aside for you. She's the best milker I have.''

' "Oh," I told him, "it doesn't matter to me who does the milking as long as I'm allowed to watch.''

'Well, you never heard such laughter. Not that I could blame Mr Corcoran for being amused. You see, it seems that Eileen was the cow, not the milker.'

There were a few suppressed giggles from us but most of us were respectfully quiet, not wanting Grand-Uncle Sopsa to think that we found his ignorance amusing. Anyway, we'd have made the same mistake ourselves.

' "No, Mr Marcus," Mr Corcoran said, "I'll attend to the milking meself.''

'I told him there was no need to trouble himself but he insisted. He said he'd be glad to do it because he had only recently put in automatic milking machines and was afraid he'd be getting out of practice in the old method. So he welcomed the chance to do some hand-milking again. He gave me directions how to find his farm – it was a few miles outside the city – and on the day before Passover I went there on the bus. When I got off the bus the conductor told me where to go and in a few minutes I was walking up the muddy track to the farm, a can in each hand, scattering chickens on my way.

'Mr Corcoran was waiting for me and he took me to a long shed – a long, noisy shed, because there was a great sound of bellowing and mooing coming from it. When Mr Corcoran opened the door, the noise almost deafened me, but he didn't seem to hear it at all. There were about thirty cows there, each in her own stall, and Mr Corcoran walked down the line until he halted at one and gave her a slap on her behind.

' "This is Eileen," he said, "the best milker of the lot."

'He took my cans from me, sat down on a stool by Eileen's side, and started to milk her. I watched him for a while until my eye was caught by the electrical machinery running along the roof.

' "Do you like the electric milker, Mr Corcoran?" I asked, just to make conversation.

' "It's all right," he said.

' "Do the cows like it?" I said.

' "Ah, that's the question now," he answered. "They didn't take to it at first. They were bad-tempered and their milk was slow and thin. But it's back to normal again, so I suppose they're getting used to it. Like their owner."

' "But will the change back to hand-milking upset Eileen?" I asked.

' "Not her," Mr Corcoran said, "nothing upsets her. Anyway, I hand-milked her this morning just to get her used to it again and I won't use the machine on her again until your Easter is over."

'The cows weren't making as much noise as I walked back to the shed door, a full can of milk in each hand. I turned to thank Mr Corcoran for his kindness but he hadn't moved from Eileen's stall. He still stood there, his head bent as if he was listening, or perhaps puzzled by something.

'On my second visit, three days later, I could see immediately that he looked worried.

' "It's just the cows," he explained. "They're a bit off colour. Milk's not the best. Except Eileen – she's still tip-top, bless her."

'But no sooner had he started milking her when he stopped and lifted his head.

' "Listen," he said. "D'you hear, Mr Marcus?"

' "What?" I asked. "I hear nothing."

' "That's it. The silence. There's not a sound from the rest of them!"

'He was right. I was so interested in watching Mr Corcoran that I hadn't noticed they had all suddenly stopped mooing.

' "What's wrong?" ' I asked.

We all leaned forward to hear the explanation. But there wasn't one. Grand-Uncle Sopsa shrugged his shoulders and continued.

' "Blessed if I know," Mr Corcoran said to me. "But it can't be much if they're not shouting about it."

'Still,' Grand-Uncle Sopsa closed one eye meditatively, 'I had the feeling that Mr Corcoran was more worried than he pretended, and on my last visit, two days later, one look at his face was enough. It was clear that all wasn't well.

' "I hope your milk will be good, Mr Marcus," he whispered to me. "They're all giving bad stuff except Eileen. And I fear she might go sour on me too."

'We went into the shed. Immediately we put our noses inside the door, the mooing stopped as if all the cows had fallen asleep at the exact same moment. I was amazed. It seemed so unnatural.

' "And that's not all," Mr Corcoran said, still whispering, as if he was afraid of something he couldn't explain. "They're acting very peculiar. Every time I turn them out, they keep away from Eileen. If she tries to go with them, they crowd together and move off. I've never seen anything like it."

' "Why should they do that?" I asked him.

'But Mr Corcoran had no idea. "I wish I knew," he said. Then he pointed to the electric milking machinery

99

above our heads. "I told you they didn't like that at first, and now that they see me hand-milking Eileen every day – well, damned if I don't think they're jealous of her and going on strike!"

'I suppose Mr Corcoran saw by the look on my face that I wasn't convinced by that story.

' "Well, what do you think yourself, Mr Marcus?" he asked.

'I knew immediately what I thought but I didn't tell Mr Corcoran.

'Antisemitism!'

Grand-Uncle Sopsa paused and looked around us to let the word sink in. We were as silent as Mr Corcoran's cows had been. We knew what antisemitism was – if not from our own experience, then from stories our parents and grandparents had told of their early life in far-off foreign lands.

'Of course,' Grand-Uncle Sopsa continued, 'whatever was troubling Mr Corcoran's cows, they got over it quickly. When he resumed delivering the milk after Passover, he told me that as soon as he returned to milking Eileen by machinery, the other cows behaved as if nothing had happened. Their milk was as good as ever and they stopped ignoring Eileen when they were all out in the field.

' "It was nothing serious after all, Mr Marcus," Mr Corcoran said.

' "No," I replied, "nothing serious."

'But I wonder. Had the cows just been trying to tell Mr Corcoran that they preferred to be hand-milked like Eileen, or was it something more than that? Could they have been jealous of Eileen because she was the Chosen Cow? What do you think, my friends?'

One winter, when some of us were still young enough to be inquisitive about Christmas and all of us were madly envious of the marvellous Christmas presents our Christian schoolmates always got, Grand-Uncle Sopsa told us the truth about Santa Claus.

100

'Of course, my friends,' he said, as the fire danced up the chimney and outside the window the early darkness hardened and grew cold, 'I'm sure you're all too grown-up now to believe in Santa Claus, not that you ever did—'

We avoided each other's eyes, anxious to conceal the doubts that even yet might be lingering in our minds. We had nothing in the Jewish calendar that could remotely compare with Christmas – *Chanukah*, the annual Festival of Lights, which fell at around the same time, was traditionally an occasion for giving children presents of small sums of money, but what were a few coins against the largesse that Christmas brought? And there was the whole atmosphere of the season – the extra-busy streets, the rows of turkeys hanging like aeroplanes nose-diving into the ground, the festooned shop windows, the carol singers surrounded by knots of smiling pedestrians and not one saying that it was wrong to be singing out of doors. In the biggest store in town Santa Claus used to make a special two-week visit, but of course we were never taken to see him. Some of us, pretending we had been invited to play in a cousin's house, once sneaked down to see what it was like. We didn't stay long. We found it too unbearable, listening to all those lucky children screaming with anticipation as they waited to whisper a few words into Santa's ear and exchange their shillings for a brightly wrapped box from his own hand. Each day at school in break time, it being too cold to go out, we sat dumbly drinking in their discussions of what each one was expecting to find in his stocking on Christmas morning. That seemed the crowning bit of magic. The only magic *we* had was the moment during the Passover *Seder* when the front door was opened for Elijah, the prophet, to come in and drink the glass of wine that had stood waiting for him all evening. But when the door was closed not a drop had ever vanished from the glass, so what sort of magic was that? It certainly couldn't hold a candle to stories we heard of how Santa Claus would come down the chimney with his bulging sack, how you had to hang up your stocking on the end of your bed the night before, how you had to be sure to be asleep or he might not leave anything for you, and then the heart-stopping miracle of waking up to find your presents there, new, sparkling, ready to be played with.

And the Christmas trees! Everywhere we went they were shining and winking at us in front windows from whose open curtains we found it impossible to avert our gaze. Behind them we often caught sight of mantelpieces crammed with Christmas cards, so many that it seemed the people who lived in the houses must have known everyone in the town and had friends all over Ireland. All over the world.

Of course it was to Santa Claus that our thoughts and dreams always returned. To us Santa Claus *was* Christmas. In our mind's eye we saw him flying through the skies in his tinkling sleigh, cheerfully noting all the houses on his list. We were reminded of the ancient Israelites enslaved in Egypt, when the Lord, visiting the ten plagues on Pharaoh and his cruel people, sent the Angel of Death to slay all the Egyptian first-born but to pass over the houses of the Children of Israel. Santa Claus was another angel who had to pass over the houses of the children of Israel, but we yearned for it to be otherwise. And the more we yearned, the more guilty we felt. So when Grand-Uncle Sopsa said that he would tell us the truth about Santa Claus, we all hoped that, if what he was going to reveal did not salve our consciences, it might at least ease our regrets.

'None of you', he commenced, 'ever knew a boy named Yankel Birzansky. It was before you were born and the Birzanskys don't live here any more. Yankel had no brothers or sisters, but he had loving parents whose greatest wish was to see him grow up into a good, strong, clever boy. Good Yankel was, though, no better, I'm sure, than any of you.' Grand-Uncle Sopsa smiled innocently, making us feel that he knew we were little devils, but harmless ones. 'And strong,' he went on, 'my goodness, Yankel was certainly big and strong. Would you believe – when he was eight, people who didn't know him thought he was twelve already. Good – strong – clever. Clever? Well, so-so. Not stupid, but not a genius. Too much of a dreamer. That worried his father, Shlomo Birzansky, because dreamers don't get very far in life. Shlomo had to work hard to make a living. "Where would we be", he said to his wife, Rachel, "if I were a dreamer?" And so Shlomo thought a lot about how to bring his son down to earth.

'Christmas, of course, meant nothing to Shlomo and Rachel. Why should it! They were good Jews, and Christmas was a Christian festival. Yankel was a good Jewish boy too – he had been going to *cheder* since he was six, he could read his Hebrew prayer-book, and already he was able to recite the *Kiddush* after his father at the commencement of the Sabbath every Friday night. But come December, all he could talk about was Christmas!'

At this we squirmed a bit in our seats and stole glances at each other. We knew exactly how Yankel Birzansky had felt.

'Now where had Yankel heard so much about Christmas?' Grand-Uncle Sopsa asked. (We knew the answer to that too.) 'In school of course, where I'm sure you hear about Christmas every year also. But Yankel wasn't like you. As I told you, he was a dreamer, and all the wonderful stories about Christmas – especially about Santa Claus – made him wish – well, not exactly that he had been a Christian, but that, even though he was a Jew, Santa Claus might be able to come down his chimney just once.'

More squirming from us. How different had we been from Yankel Birzansky, we asked ourselves.

' "What will we do with him, Rachel?" Shlomo appealed. "What will become of our son? How can we make him realize that he can't dream his way through life? All this talk about Christmas and Santa Claus. . . ."'

'Rachel didn't share her husband's worries. Yankel would surely grow out of his childish dreams. Another

103

year or two and Christmas and Santa Claus would mean nothing to him. Shlomo was a good man but he expected too much too soon. Time enough to be strict with their son. He was still only a big baby.'

Grand-Uncle Sopsa shrugged, as if to let us know that he neither agreed nor disagreed with Rachel Birzansky. But we guessed that Shlomo hadn't agreed with his wife, and we were right.

'Shlomo looked at his "big baby" and shook his head. A few years' time might be too late. Already nature had developed his body but it hadn't developed his mind. His parents would have to do that. Shlomo looked again at his son and made his decision. It was time to act.

' "My son," he said, one very cold day a week before Christmas when the skies were dark and Yankel was gazing out the window at the falling snow, "I have a surprise for you."

'Yankel looked up in wonderment. Or perhaps I should say that he looked down in wonderment, for already he was bigger than his father.'

We laughed uproariously. Grand-Uncle Sopsa's joke helped break the tension of waiting to hear what Shlomo Birzansky was going to do.

' "A surprise?" Yankel said. "What is it, *Tata*?"

'Rachel Birzansky said nothing. She wasn't happy with her husband's plan.

' "This year, Yankel," Shlomo said, and he paused a moment to make his announcement more dramatic, "this year we are going to celebrate Christmas."

'Yankel looked at his father but he didn't utter a word. He thought he must not have heard properly or else that his father had suddenly lost his senses.

'Shlomo Birzansky was disappointed. He had expected shouts of joy, wild excitement, perhaps even a little dance, but instead all he got was silence and a puzzled stare.

' "Christmas," he repeated. "You know what Christmas is. You talk enough about it. Well, we're going to have Christmas this year, in this house, and you can do all the things that your Christian schoolfriends do at Christmas. What do you say to that?''

' "But *Tata* . . .," was all Yankel could say.

' "I know what you're thinking," his father told him. "You're thinking Christmas is a Christian festival, so how can a Jew observe it?"

'Yankel nodded.

' "Why not?" Shlomo continued. "Nothing in the five books of Moses says we can't celebrate Christmas. It's supposed to be a season of goodwill. Well, Abraham, Isaac, Jacob, Moses – they were all men of goodwill. Can a good Jew not join in such a celebration?''

' "You mean Santa Claus would be able to come down our chimney?" Yankel asked doubtfully.

' "How else would he bring your presents?''

' "Presents!" Yankel's thoughts were beginning to race with visions of the wonderful toys he could get.

' "You will write Santa Claus a letter," Shlomo declared, "just as all your schoolfriends do, telling him what presents you want – only remember, don't be greedy, he has millions of other children to consider. We'll have a Christmas tree, and on Christmas Eve you'll hang up your stocking before you go to bed, and while you're asleep, Santa Claus will come. Yes?''

'Yankel looked towards his mother for confirmation. He still could not believe it. Something would go wrong or his father would change his mind. Rachel looked back at him. There were tears in her eyes. He thought they must be tears of happiness for his good fortune.

'He got busy immediately. Almost crying with anticipation and excitement he got pen and ink, tore a clean white page from his school jotter, and sat down with his father to write his letter to Santa Claus.

'It turned out that it wasn't as easy a letter to write as he had imagined. There were so many toys and games he wanted to have. That was the difficulty – choosing between them, because he couldn't ask for them all.'

We nodded. We understood how difficult his problem

was – not that we would have minded having such a problem ourselves.

'At last, with his father's help, he decided on three presents, three presents so wonderful, so alluring, that never in his wildest dreams had he seen himself as one day possessing them. They were a Hornby train set complete with passenger carriages, Pullman cars, wagons, stations, bridges, viaducts, signals, and water tanks; a Number Seven Meccano set; and a fountain pen to make him the envy of every boy in his class. He blotted the letter carefully, put it in an envelope, addressed it, and gave it to his father to post. Shlomo Birzansky solemnly put the letter in his pocket and said he would post it that very day. Rachel stood by. She said nothing. She felt sad, but she still said nothing.

'When Shlomo returned from his store that evening, Yankel ran up to him excitedly to ask if his letter had been posted, but when he saw what his father had brought home he could only stand dumbly and gaze in awe. A Christmas tree! A real, magical, spell-binding Christmas tree! And a box of faery lights, all colours of the rainbow, to make it sparkle and glow just the same as all the other Christmas trees in the road! Yankel insisted that they put it up immediately, without even waiting until they had their tea, so he and his father set to work and in no time at all the tree was standing in all its glory, its lights shining and winking on the outstretched branches. But there was one thing missing. Yankel and his father looked at each other. Both of them knew what it was.

' "But we can't put an angel on the top," Shlomo said. "Jews don't have angels."

' "Some trees have stars, *Tata*," Yankel answered. "Couldn't we just have a star?"

'Shlomo's eyes lit up, almost as brightly as the sparkling lights. A star! The very thing!

'Quickly he cut out a star from a big piece of card, coloured it blue and white, the Jewish colours, and pinned it proudly to the top of the tree.

106

' "There," he said, stepping back to admire his work, "*Magen David*, the Star of David, the emblem of the Jews. Now that's *really* a Jewish Christmas tree!"

'Yankel laughed and laughed. His mother saw his joy and her heart was heavy.

'Over the next few days Yankel's excitement kept growing until by the time Christmas Eve arrived he couldn't sit still for a single moment. But for Rachel it was otherwise. With Shlomo out at work all day, it was to her that her son brought all his questions. She tried her best to explain what Christmas was supposed to mean. But when he asked about Santa Claus – as he increasingly did – she was lost for answers. What could she say to him when he wondered where Santa Claus lived, when he said that surely it must be impossible to ride through the skies behind a team of reindeer, when he protested that even if Santa Claus *could* succeed in making such a miraculous journey, how in the world could he manage to come down a narrow chimney with a bulging sack on his back? Wouldn't he get stuck? And there was the question he kept coming back to, the one that completely defeated him – and completely defeated all Rachel's attempts to explain away: how could three stores – *three* stores – in the same town possibly have Santa Claus visit them *all at the same time*?

'She was glad when Christmas Eve came – glad because soon the whole business would be finished with. She expected that Christmas Day, and the few days afterwards, would bring her a greater trial, but at least it would be the sort of trial a mother was used to – that of comforting her heart-broken child when one of his most precious dreams has been shattered.'

At this point Grand-Uncle Sopsa left us for a moment to step into the kitchen for a drink of water, but we were all so spellbound by the story of Yankel Birzansky and Santa Claus that not one of us said a word or even moved a muscle while he was gone. When he returned, he settled himself, coughed, and then went on.

'Yankel was allowed to stay up late on the big night – anyway he was much too excited for bed, and Shlomo wanted to make sure his son would not stay awake too long but would quickly fall into a heavy sleep. He helped him hang up his stocking, explaining that of course the big presents wouldn't fit in it but that Santa would leave them at the foot of the bed and probably leave a small, special gift in the stocking. Then Rachel said good night to her son, holding him close to her bosom until he had to struggle to free himself so that he could lie back, bury his head in his pillow, and have the great adventure begin. Together his parents left the room, closing the door quietly behind them.

'Mr and Mrs Birzansky sat side by side in their kitchen for the next few hours, not speaking. Shlomo knew how much his wife disapproved of what he was doing but he told himself that sometimes a parent has to be cruel to be kind. Rachel gazed for a long time at the faery lights winking on the Christmas tree until they appeared to be mocking her. She got up and switched them off. There had never been Christmas in the Birzansky home and there never would be – least of all for her son.

'Her action seemed to awaken Shlomo and remind him of what he had to do. She watched him take a small white card from his wallet and write something on it. She did not have to read what he had written. She knew what it was: *Santa Claus does not exist.*

' "It is time," he said. "He should be well asleep by now."

'She nodded. They both rose. She followed him to her son's bedroom.

'Soundlessly Shlomo Birzansky opened the door a few inches and peeped in. In the darkness he could just make out a humped figure in the bed. It was quite motionless. Yankel was fast asleep.'

Grand-Uncle Sopsa paused. We held our breath.

'Slowly Shlomo pushed the door open wide enough for him to creep into the room. His wife did not follow him.

She waited outside, her back to the door, her eyes closed tight to stifle her sorrow.

'Like a ghost, Shlomo tiptoed across the floor towards the end of Yankel's bed. He had to grope along it to find the stocking hanging there, limp and empty. Into it he dropped his card: *Santa Claus does not exist.* Then, as silently as he had come, he turned and tiptoed back towards the door.

'He had just reached the threshold when suddenly some huge object rose up from behind the door and threw itself at him. With a crash Shlomo was knocked flying. His elbow hit the floor and his head hit the wall so hard that he thought it would burst open. "I've got him, I've got him," the object cried, "I've caught Santa Claus."

' "Help! Help! I'm murdered!" Shlomo shrieked as Rachel Birzansky rushed in and switched on the light. She found her husband stretched on the ground, trying to hold his reeling head in his hands and rub his elbow at the same time. Beside him was her son. In the bed the pillow had been bundled up under the covers to look like a sleeping figure.

' "Yankel, Yankel," Rachel cried, "it's not Santa Claus. It's your father."

' "I know," Yankel laughed. "I knew all the time."

'Shlomo Birzansky stopped nursing his wounds and stared at his son. "You knew?"

' "Of course I knew. I've known for years."

' "How did you find out?" his father asked.

' "The boys at school told me. They know it's their fathers put the presents in their stockings but they pretend it's Santa Claus so as to keep getting presents every Christmas."

'Yankel turned to look for the presents he believed his father had brought. Seeing no Hornby train set, no box of Meccano, he went to the hanging stocking and peered into it. He took out the card nestling inside and read it. Silently he turned to his parents, his eyes clouded with disappointment, his lip quivering.

'Rachel had helped her husband to his feet and they both stood looking at their son. He was doing his best to keep back his tears. Shlomo was still rubbing his head, trying to soothe his pain.

' "Come," Rachel said, taking his arm. "It's late and Yankel must get some sleep. I'll put some lint on your elbow and when you lie down you'll feel much better."

'She pushed Shlomo out of the room, but before closing the door she slipped a hand into her apron pocket and drew from it a sparkling silver fountain pen. She held it out to Yankel. In an instant the tears were banished and his eyes lit up with joy. A fountain pen! Now he'd be the only boy in his class with a fountain pen. He took it in his hands and kissed his mother.

' "I hope *Tata* will be all right," he said. "I hope I didn't hurt him."

' "Only his pride, Yankel, only his pride," she whispered. "But he'll get over it."

'Later, when husband and wife were lying together in bed, Rachel said, "You see, my man, our son isn't stupid. He isn't such a dreamer after all."

' "You mean because he knew about Santa Claus? Because he was only pretending to believe in him?"

' "Not only that, wise one. Didn't you notice that he waited until you had put something in his stocking before knocking you down. Clever boy! He wasn't going to attack Santa Claus until *after* he'd had a chance to deliver his presents."

'In the darkness Shlomo Birzansky thought about what his wife had said. After a while he smiled happily to himself and turned on his side to go to sleep. His elbow no longer ached, his head had stopped throbbing, and perhaps his son would turn out to be as clever as his father after all!'

It was usual for all of us to drop out of Grand-Uncle Sopsa's story circle once we reached the age of twelve. At that point the girls were beginning to turn into young

110

ladies and we boys – starting to prepare for our *Bar Mitzvah* – into young men. Of course I saw a good deal of him after that, but, already trying to put childhood associations behind me, I paid him scant attention. So there were no more stories. Not, that is, until I was seventeen.

I had just got the results of my national Intermediate Certificate examination and the bottom had fallen out of my world. I had thought I would do well, very well, might even win a scholarship to go to university – but my marks were much lower than expected. The idea of a repeat year in school – if I wanted to try again for the scholarship – horrified me. I was completely disillusioned with the whole business of school, university, studies, education in general, and I went around in a thoroughly sullen, resentful, morose mood.

It was then that Grand-Uncle Sopsa sent for me. I hadn't seen him for a while because he had been ill, very ill in fact. When I went to his room he was sitting in a chair by his bed. He looked so different – instead of the pinstripe suit he was in pyjamas and a dressing-gown, instead of the sparkling boots and spats his feet were in carpet slippers. But the familiar grey Homburg was still on his head and to some extent that helped off-set the almost frightening pallor of his skin.

He asked me how I felt and, selfishly, I told him. I poured out all my disgust, self-pity, disillusionment, truculence. I told him that obviously school had been largely a waste of time and university would only be more of the same. I told him that I had worked hard for the examination but still hadn't got the result I deserved, and I implied that there was something unfair about it all, that life was being particularly cruel to me. If that was how things were going to be, then I didn't want any part of them.

He let me rant on, nodding his head now and again or sometimes shaking it slowly from side to side in sympathy. When I was quite finished, he closed his eyes for a moment, then opened them again and looked fully at me.

111

'*Dovidil*,' he said, using the pet version of my Hebrew name, something he had never used before and which even my parents had stopped calling me years earlier.

'*Dovidil*,' he repeated, 'let me tell you a story. It's a true story, one that really happened, not like the other ones I just make up.'

He smiled shyly, and the intimacy of the smile, the quite deliberate revelation in his admission about all the other stories he had told in his life – both to children and to adults – shocked me out of my own self-absorption and made me listen with all the old rapt attention. I'm glad I did, for it was the very last story poor Grand-Uncle Sopsa ever told. He died the next day. No doubt the breaking of that special link with my childhood helped me to grow up, but it was the story that brought me to my senses.

Here it is.

'You were too young at the time to remember Buldings,' he commenced. 'It was only a few years after the war and he appeared in our community quite suddenly. One day he wasn't here, next day he was. Of course "Buldings" wasn't his real name. I've forgotten what *that* was – something very difficult to pronounce and very difficult to remember. Even more foreign than some of our own names. He had learned a little English – not much, but enough to make himself understood. Why do I call him "Buldings"? I'll tell you.

'The day after he arrived was Sabbath and someone brought him to *shul*. You know our synagogue – small, shabby, it was shabby then and it's still shabby now – and almost beside it is that big church. Well, he stood in the road and looked at the *shul*, then he looked at the church, then he looked again at the *shul*.

' "Ach," he said at last, "very nice, very goot. Brother and sister. No? No. Father and son. Two beautiful buldings."

'From then on he was known as "Buldings".

'Of course Buldings couldn't stay long in our community. He had no money, no job, no prospect of one, and

112

nowhere to live. The Board of Guardians knew that once he had had a bit of a rest, they'd have to give him his fare to Dublin or London. In the meantime, until they could hold a meeting to interview him and discuss his case, they paid for his lodgings and gave him a little money to buy food.

'But Buldings was no beggar. He had a big portmanteau with him that he dragged about everywhere. It was almost as big as himself, battered and dirty, with old torn labels all over it. In it he had a collection of goods and at any opportunity he'd snap the case open and try to sell you a packet of razor blades or a bundle of laces or a cheap ash-tray. And he always asked questions, all sorts of questions. But after his meeting with the Board of Guardians there was one particular question that kept worrying him for the rest of the few days he was here.

'At the meeting with the officers of the Board, they listened to his story of suffering. It was the sort of story they had heard before from other survivors of the concentration camps, a story of homelessness and years of aimless wandering. Buldings told them about the horrors he had witnessed and the family he had lost. He had some old documents that were so faded no one could read them – something to do with his qualifications it seemed – and even a photograph of his wife and children that somehow – God knows how – he had managed to save through it all. *Gevald, gevald*, it was so tragic. He had been helped everywhere, he said – helped to keep wandering.

'The President of the Board, a barrister, spoke kindly to Buldings, explaining the difficulties of small communities in dealing with displaced persons. Buldings was bewildered by the strange phrase. It was new to him. He looked up questioningly.

' "I am a displeased person?" he asked.

The officers laughed and the barrister tried to explain.

' "No, no. I didn't say a displeased person. And I hope your troubles haven't turned you into a cynic."

'The barrister continued his homily but Buldings heard

113

no more. The strange words had stuck in his thoughts, and as soon as the interview was over, he buttonholed the first member of the community he could find.

' ''Please,'' he said, ''you tell me. From vot is a chinnick?''

'The congregant happened to be old Ross, the antique dealer, and he was too busy to listen to Buldings' question. Anyway, he probably wouldn't have known the answer. But Buldings had to keep trying. He asked the community secretary, but the secretary's definition was too fumbling for Buldings to understand. He asked the minister, but the minister's explanation was so full of Talmudical examples that Buldings' brain reeled. Still he persevered, and overnight ''From vot is a chinnick?'' became a standing joke in the community. We were all amused – all except Buldings. He shuffled about, dragging his suitcase after him, seeking an answer to his question.

'Then a few days later, while I was reading in the local library, Buldings appeared at the door. His eyes lit up when he recognized me and he tiptoed over to my chair.

' ''Please,'' he whispered, ''I was told someone here would tell me from vot is a chinnick.''

' ''Someone here?'' I asked in surprise.

' ''Yes. Someone with name Dick something. Dick Shunry? You know him here?''

' ''Not a person,'' I explained, barely able to check my laughter, ''a thing. A dictionary.''

' ''Yes. You know him?''

' ''I know him,'' I agreed. ''Here he is.''

'I left my chair and went to a shelf for a dictionary. With Buldings peering around my arm I brought the volume back to the desk and helped him find his word.

' ''Ach,'' he exclaimed in delight as my finger pinpointed it, ''a chinnick!''

'He read the definition: *One of a sect founded by Antisthenes of Athens (born c.444 BC), characterized by an ostentatious contempt for riches, arts, science, etc. – so called from their morose manners.*

'He read it again, a number of times. It was clear that he had no idea what it meant. His eyes appealed to me.

' "Come on, Buldings," I said. "I'll explain it to you."

'I took him to a little restaurant next door and over a cup of coffee I explained the definition to him word by word.

'He listened silently, and when I finished with "And that's the meaning of a *cynic*," he sat forward anxiously.

' "It is wrong," he protested. "I am not a chinnick. I am not, what you say, marrows."

' "Morose," I corrected. "A displeased person. Aren't you displeased? After all your troubles and wandering, don't you feel any contempt for riches, arts, science?"

' "Yes," he admitted. "Yes, I do. The rich men – have they time for me? The arts – have I time for them? And science – look what killings it has made in the world. But displeased, me? No, not. Without science I would have no little razor blades to sell and get some money; without the arts and learning you would not have found for me that big book to tell me from vot is a chinnick; and without rich men there might be no Board of Guardians to help me. So I am not displeased. I am not a chinnick."

' "You certainly aren't," I laughed. "I think you're more of a philosopher than a cynic."

' "Goot," he said as we got up. I paid the bill and led Buldings to the door.

'Outside the restaurant I was saying goodbye when he put a hand on my arm.

' "Excuse," he said. "You forgive me to delay you. But please to tell me – from vot is a philotchofer?" '

The Clanbrassil Bagel

Sol Wise paid his annual dues to the New York Yiddish
Sons of St Patrick and every year on 17th March he put on
his green beret and green tie, pinned a monster sprig of
shamrock to his lapel, took his miniature tricolour in
hand and marched proudly up Fifth Avenue in the St
Patrick's Day Parade.

Not that Sol Wise was Irish – or indeed had ever been to
the country – but his mother was. And to his mother,
Esther Eisenberg, Sol owed everything – to her and to her
recipe for the bagel, the Jewish doughnut.

Esther Eisenberg had been born Esther Rubinstein on
January 1st, 1900, at No. 63 Clanbrassil Street, Dublin.
Clanbrassil Street was at the time the heart of Dublin's
Jewish quarter, a narrow street to which the hundreds of
Jews fleeing from persecution in Poland and Russia and
Lithuania came and made their own. Esther grew up
there, went to school to the nuns in the Catholic convent
nearby, went to *cheder* to learn her Hebrew prayers in
Rabbi Levy's dingy back room, and at dawn every Monday listened to the clip-clop of horses' hooves as the
viklaniks, the weekly traders, loaded their store of fancy
goods into their traps to peddle them to the villagers and
farmers' wives of Kildare, Meath and Wicklow, and any
other place they could reach and get back from by Friday
evening for the Sabbath. She knew intimately most of the
families in Clanbrassil Street and she could name all its
little shops – the *kosher* butchers, the hucksters, the chand-
lers with the miniature coloured candles for *Hanukah*,

117

the phylactery and religious books sellers, the provision shops where Jewish delicacies like chopped liver, pickled herring, *matzo* and special biscuits for Passover as well as *hamantash* for Purim could be obtained. She also knew the Jewish bakers to which the inhabitants flocked for the dark, almost black Jewish rye bread, for the plaited white *challah* that would grace the Sabbath table, and for bagels.

There were, in fact, only three Jewish bakers in Clanbrassil Street, and while the other two managed to make a living, it was Rubinstein's, Esther's parents' establishment, that most of the Jewish housewives patronized. The attraction was Mrs Rubinstein's bagels – they were something special, famed throughout the length and breadth of Clanbrassil Street, wholesome and munchy when – in keeping with the dietary laws – taken dry with meat, divinely succulent and toothsome when butter-soaked for the milk meal. They were baked every day – except on the Sabbath, of course – for breakfast table, dinner and supper, and extra supplies were baked on Sunday to sustain the *viklaniks* during their expeditions to the country. Somehow, was it the result of some special ingredient or the Hebrew blessing Mrs Rubinstein intoned over them, the travellers' supplies seemed to stay fresh and pulpy well into the week.

Esther, of course, worked in the bakery after school, but when she left school her parents decided that they wanted a better future for her than working in a bakery all her life, so they gave her a little money, some food, and a bag of bagels, and sent her off to relations in New York to find her fortune there, or if not a fortune, perhaps fame – and if neither, a husband at least. The last Esther did find, and quickly. At the age of sixteen she married Percy Eisenberg, at seventeen Sol was born to them, and at eighteen Percy walked out and was never heard from again. In truth Esther didn't greatly miss him for he had been a shiftless, soft-soaping con-man who had talked her into marrying him and who had objected to her calling him Piaras – which she told him was the Irish version of his name – rather than Percy. After he disappeared she had been heard to say that anyone who preferred 'Percy' to 'Piaras' couldn't be up to much anyway.

The years of Sol's childhood and youth were difficult ones for him and his mother. There were plenty of jobs she could get in New York and she tried most of them – waitress, cigarette girl, seamstress, usherette – but none of them paid well and the hours were long or unsocial or both. The little time she could spend in her two rented rooms were devoted to caring and cooking for her child. She constantly told him stories of her life in Clanbrassil Street, Dublin, until he knew what the street looked like almost as well as she did, and she cooked for him all the Jewish dishes and delicacies her own mother had cooked for her. His favourite was her bagels – she had inherited from her mother the special gift of producing a bagel that no one else could match – and it was those selfsame bagels that were to become the foundation of his life's success and wealth.

How it came about was that in all the jobs Sol had in his teens – and they were many – he always took a bag of Esther's bagels to sustain him through the day. Frequently he would share them with his workmates, who invariably found them irresistible and vowed they were the best bagels in New York. Indeed, so ecstatic were their praises and so all-consuming their demand for Esther Eisenberg's bagels, that Sol thought it might be a good idea to try selling them. First he placed a few dozen in a friend's street stall. They were bought and devoured within minutes. The next night he brought along double the number and they, too, went in no time – most of them to satisfied customers who had bought them on the previous night and had avidly come back for more. Quick to spot a money-spinner, he persuaded his mother to stay home for a week and bake, while he went out, hired a stall of his own, and filled it with her bagels. He painted his name on the stall but 'Eisenberg's Bagels' seemed to lack the zip he wanted,

119

so he changed his name to Wise, called his stall The Wise Bagel, and the enterprise took off. Within months Wise Bagel stalls were all over the city, he had won concessions to supply the bagels to many of the top restaurants and hotels, and Esther was happily working full-time to keep pace with the orders. When people asked him for his bagel recipe he ungrudgingly gave it. Indeed, so confident was he that no one could rival his mother's bagels that he pinned up the recipe outside all his stalls with the offer – 'If *you* can bake a better bagel, I'll buy it.' Nobody could. Within a few years there were branches of The Wise Bagel in most of the big cities along the east coast with plans to spread west, there was a huge bagel factory closely supervised by Esther, and Sol and his mother had become the toast of the media with their picture on the cover of *Time* magazine and more fame and wealth than they could dream of.

In due course Sol got married – though, sadly, family history repeated itself, in reverse, for after producing a son, his wife (who had never liked bagels) left him for a pumpernickel prince, and Sol moved back with his offspring to the sumptuous apartment he had bought for Esther.

Year overtook year with Sol and his mother growing ever more prosperous. They holidayed in Miami, Vegas, Acapulco; they visited Disneyland; and when Sol's son, Lennie, grew up and graduated from business college, Sol made him Vice-President in Charge of Operations at The Wise Bagel so he and Esther could have even more time off. Strangely, however, even though Esther continually reminisced about her youth in Ireland and told Sol story after story of her days in No. 63 Clanbrassil Street, Dublin, they never went there for a holiday. Perhaps Esther was afraid that to go back might in some way spoil her memories, so every year she vowed she would go 'next year'. 'Next year', however, never comes round; what did come round, before Esther could fulfil her vow, was her death. On 1st January 1980, she passed away peacefully in her sleep.

Sol was distraught, utterly lost without the mother he had adored. For months afterwards he would remain hunched in an armchair in the sitting-room, eyeing the urn holding her ashes which he had installed on a marble pedestal in a humidity-free glass case, remembering all the wonderful years she had spent in Clanbrassil Street, Dublin, before he was born.

While he languished, Lennie competently managed The Wise Bagel until eventually Sol recovered some of his former zest and began to formulate schemes to spread the business throughout the world. His most ambitious brainwave was to flood Russia with Wise bagels.

'But, Pop,' Lennie remonstrated, 'if the Russians won't even let the Jews out, how do you expect them to let bagels in?'

'*Schmuck,*' his father replied, 'if the Russians let the bagels in, then the Jews won't want to get out' – an argument which, unfortunately, failed to convince the Soviet authorities.

He launched a nationwide advertising campaign for which he thought up slogans. The one he was most proud of was 'Go to bed with a bagel' and posters carrying that advice appeared all over the US with a witty Thurber-like illustration to make people laugh.

Deep down, however, Sol was unhappy. Something was bugging him, something he couldn't quite identify. Eventually it hit him – Clanbrassil Street, Dublin! Neither his mother – or at least her ashes – nor he could rest happy until he had been to Clanbrassil Street, Dublin, and paid tribute there to Esther's memory. He'd put a plaque on No. 63 – yes, that was it, he'd put a plaque on No. 63.

Sol Wise hadn't got where he was by hanging around and the very next day he hopped on a plane, landed at Dublin Airport, and took a taxi straight to Clanbrassil Street.

What he saw surprised and shocked him. What surprised him was that Clanbrassil Street was a much shorter street than he had expected. Still, that figured; childhood memories of places always made them larger than life. No doubt with all the Jewish families there at the time and their shops and businesses, it must have seemed like a whole world. But what shocked him was that the shops and businesses, apart from one *kosher* butcher, had disappeared. Worse still, so much of the whole area was derelict, falling to pieces, uninhabited. No. 63, the hallowed site of his mother's birth, was a ruin with barely a wall standing, unrecognizable as a former habitation, much less as the forerunner of The Wise Bagel.

Sol was shattered. He went straight back to Dublin Airport and took the first plane home to New York.

On his return Lennie tried to comfort him.

'Whaddya expect, Pop? Jeez, it's been nearly a century since Grandma left Ireland. Whaddya expect? That the place wouldn't change?'

'Change, yes,' Sol accepted. 'But not that it would decay, just die. You shoulda seen it, Lennie. I can't describe it. Thank God your grandmother never went back. It would have broken her heart.'

'Well, now *you've* seen it, Pop, you can forget it, yeah?' Lennie asked anxiously.

Forget it, no. Sol wished he could, but it kept nagging at him. Esther, too, kept nagging at him – her memories, her stories, her deep love for her Irish heritage. He became obsessed by the idea that somehow he had to find a way of honouring her birth at No. 63 Clanbrassil Street, Dublin. Sure, but what sort of *schmuck* would be stoopid enough to put a plaque on a derelict site where no one came and where in no time at all it would probably fall into the rubble and be lost for ever?

And then, one wet day in 1987, he spotted a short paragraph in the *New York Times* reporting that in 1988 Dublin, Ireland, would be one thousand years old and special events and festivals were being planned for the whole year to celebrate the city's millennium.

Elated, he rushed to show Lennie the report.

'I got it, son, I got it!'

'Whatcha got, Pop?'

'Your grandmother – Clanbrassil Street. I'll buy Number Sixty-three, we'll build a factory there, have a gala opening during the millennium and flood Ireland with bagels.'

Lennie looked at his father, his eyes clouded with doubt.

'But, Pop, I don't think there are many Jews left in Ireland any more. And supposing the Irish don't like bagels?'

'Not like your grandmother's bagels!' The thought was preposterous. 'Besides, we'll do something special for Ireland. We'll make bagels in the shape of shamrocks. She'd have loved that, Esther would.'

Lennie was appalled. His business-college grey cells clicked relentlessly.

'Pop, hold on a minute, Pop. Look at the expense, the special machinery you'd need for shamrock-shaped bagels. You'd have no margin left. It's crazy!'

'OK, son,' Sol agreed, no keener than Lennie was to lose his margin. 'Then how about this: put a shamrock into every hundredth bag and any customer who finds a shamrock in his bag of bagels gets free bagels for a year. How about that!'

How about that indeed, thought Lennie, but he knew nothing he could say would dissuade his father. And sure enough, next day there was Sol Wise hopping a plane again to Dublin and within hours he was once more in Clanbrassil Street, sitting in the back of a taxi, surveying No. 63.

Nothing had changed. Indeed the place was more derelict than ever. That pleased him. It meant it would still be up for grabs and pricewise he'd get it for a song.

'My mother was born there,' he announced proudly to the taxi driver. 'Right there in Number Sixty-three, on the first of January, nineteen hundred.'

'Yeah?' the driver replied. He tried to show interest but he was tired after being on the night shift and not in the mood for chit-chat with yet another Yank back in Ireland to research his roots.

'Yeah,' Sol repeated. 'So you know what I'm gonna do? I'm gonna buy this darned place and build a factory right there.'

'You are?' the driver said. Sol was too wrapped up in his dream to catch the note of scepticism.

'Sure I am. For the millennium. That's what brought me over, son. Say, you don't happen to know who owns this place?'

'Well, as a matter of fact I do,' the taxi driver admitted. He meant to sound sympathetic, even commiserating, but again Sol didn't notice. To him it was a great slice of luck to be getting his first piece of vital information so easily. It hadn't struck him that Dublin taxi drivers would be as smart as New York ones.

'You do? That's great, kid. Who's the owner then? Where can I find him?'

'It's not a him,' the driver replied tersely. 'It's Dublin Corporation.'

Sol was completely nonplussed. 'Dublin Corporation? You mean like the City Council?'

'Yeah, that's right.'

'What the heck does Dublin Corporation want with a falling-down place like this, for God's sake?'

'Well, I'll tell yah,' the driver confided, 'pop' he added, thinking that a little Americanization might break the news more gently. 'The Corporation has bought all this place and they're going to send in the bulldozers and then build an eight-lane highway right through here.'

'Clanbrassil Street's goin' to be an eight-lane highway! My mother's home will be bulldozed!' Sol exploded, forgetting that time had already levelled it anyway. 'But when are they goin' to do all this? They can't have it ready for your millennium next year, that's for sure.'

'That's for sure for sure,' the taxi driver agreed. 'It probably won't even be started for years because of local opposition. Even when the plans are finalized there'll be appeals, court cases, more public inquiries maybe, the lot. Sure, it'll be years before this highway is built.'

Frustrated once again in his grand design for a memorial to his mother, Sol, for the second time, flew straight back to New York.

When he told Lennie what he had learned, his son sympathized with him, though he was secretly relieved the era of the shamrock bagel was not in fact about to dawn. Still, if he thought his father would now give up, he was mistaken. Sol Wise was determined that somehow Clanbrassil Street and his mother's memory would be joined together in a perpetual tribute.

'I got it, I got it this time,' he announced after some months' further thought. 'I've cracked it, son.'

'I'm listening, Pop,' Lennie said fearfully.

'Your grandmother was born on January One, nineteen hundred, and she passed away on January One, nineteen eighty. Yeah?'

'Yes, Pop.'

'OK. January One, two thousand, will be the hundredth anniversary of her birth. Right?'

'Right, Pop.'

'On that day, son, I'm gonna take your grandmother's ashes, fly to Dublin, go straight to Clanbrassil Street, scatter the ashes on that new highway and drive over them so that they become part of Clanbrassil Street for ever.'

Lennie looked at his father in sheer disbelief.

'You're going to do that on the first of January, two thousand, Pop?'

'Sure am. On her centenary. The new highway is bound to be ready by then. How's that, son?'

'Well, sure, Pop, that's great. But there's one snag.'

'What's that? What snag?' Sol's Irish was up and he was ready to take on whatever new obstacle might threaten.

'Well, Pop, January One, two thousand, is twelve years away. On my life, Pop, I don't wish you any ill but – well, supposing you're not here in twelve years' time. Supposing you're—' Lennie didn't dare say the word.

But Sol was no whit discouraged. 'In that case, son, *you'll* take that plane to Dublin and *you'll* make that drive down Clanbrassil Street – but with *two* urns. That's my boy.'

Next day Lennie paid a rare visit to the Temple to pray that his father should live for another twelve years – at least.

A LAND IN FLAMES
by David Marcus

It is the summer of 1920 and Ireland is in turmoil. The British army and the Black and Tans are at war with Sinn Fein – and the mainly Catholic Royal Irish Constabulary is caught in the middle . . .

Sergeant Driscoll, the loyal chief of the police station in Gortnahinch, maintains a delicate balance between his private sympathies and his public duty, but his position is continually undermined by the actions of Ambrose Mercer, the ruthless and embittered manager of Odron House and its estates, who takes pleasure in provoking the local tenantry to the point of open rebellion. Mercer is determined to get his hands on the Odron land and has embarked on a torrid affair with the eldest daughter of the house, the amoral Elizabeth. Her mother Amelia, a virtual recluse since the death of her much-loved husband, is powerless to stop Mercer in his relentless ambition, for he has a strong and shameful hold over her neither of them will ever forget . . .

Against this colourful and dramatic background David Marcus unfolds a mesmerizing story of love and loyalty, villainy and hate.

'SPLENDID ENTERTAINMENT'
Sean McMahon, IRISH INDEPENDENT

0 552 13405 8

A LAND NOT THEIRS
by David Marcus

'A whale of a book; every mark of a bestseller is here'
Terence de Vere White, THE IRISH TIMES

Set in Cork during the troubled early years of the 1920s, A
LAND NOT THEIRS is a sweeping evocation of the men
and women who made modern Ireland. Concentrating on
the tiny Jewish community in the city, the book focuses on
the increasing violence of those years and how the self-
contained Jewish community was gradually dragged into
the storm that was about to sweep Ireland. In the charged
political climate, rebellion was inevitable; as the native
Irish rose up against the hated Black and Tans the Cork
Jews found themselves drawn further and further into the
struggle for freedom and national identity.

Against the dramatic and colourful backdrop of Ireland
as it was, David Marcus, one of the country's most promi-
nent literary figures, has created unforgettable characters
and incidents which will remain in the reader's mind long
after the closing of this remarkable novel.

**'It is extremely readable and engrossing and the writing
talent shines'**
JEWISH GAZETTE

**'It is all here in *A Land Not Theirs:* the interlaced light and
shade of community living. The author has created characters that fire the imagination, a story-line that is utterly
convincing with an unerring feel both for the various dia-
lects and historical background. It is a memorable book,
one that will improve on reading a second time'**
Maureen Fox, THE CORK EXAMINER

0 552 130915

A SELECTED LIST OF TITLES
AVAILABLE FROM CORGI

☐	13359 0	**THE TENANTS OF TIME (30)**	*Thomas Flanagan* £4.99
☐	13091 5	**A LAND NOT THEIRS (50)**	*David Marcus* £3.50
☐	13405 8	**A LAND IN FLAMES (60)**	*David Marcus* £3.99
☐	99143 0	**CELTIC DAWN (28) (B)**	*Ulick O'Connor* £4.95
☐	10565 1	**TRINITY (20)**	*Leon Uris* £3.99
☐	98013 7	**IRELAND, A TERRIBLE BEAUTY (20)**	*Leon Uris* £9.75
☐	13337 X	**THE PROVISIONAL IRA (50)**	*Patrick Bishop & Eamonn Mallie* £4.99